Hallie's Heart

**Center Point
Large Print**

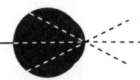

**This Large Print Book carries the
Seal of Approval of N.A.V.H.**

Hallie's Heart

Shelly Beach

CENTER POINT PUBLISHING
THORNDIKE, MAINE

Library of Congress Cataloging-in-Publication Data

Beach, Shelly.
    Hallie's heart / Shelly Beach.
        p. cm.
    ISBN 978-1-60285-697-4 (library binding : alk. paper)
    1. Michigan--Fiction. 2. Large type books. I. Title.
    PS3602.E23H35 2010
    813'.6--dc22
2009042272

For my children,
Jessica and Nathan,
who have gifted me with joy.

Acknowledgments

My sincere thanks to the many people who helped make this book a reality:

To Steve Barclift, managing editor at Kregel, who has made this journey a delight.

To editor Becky Durost Fish, who saw beyond my words and gave both wise counsel and warm encouragement.

To marketing director Dave Hill, who first caught my vision for this story and brought it back to Kregel. I owe you many more scones, Dave.

To my enormously loving and supportive family. To my parents, Paul and Phyllis Burke, who gave me a love for words, a heart for people, and a passion for God. To my children, Jessica and Nathan, who have taught me that real faith does not come prepackaged. And to my husband, Dan, who has shown endless support and patience. Words cannot express how grateful I am for your devotion and for pressing me to pursue my writing. I am above all women blessed.

To my dear writer friends, the wonderful women of the Guild—Ann Byle, Lorilee Craker, Tracy Groot, Cynthia Beach, Angela Blycker, Katrina DeMan, Julie Johnson, Jen Abbas, Alison Hodgson, and Sharon Carrns. God backed up His heavenly Mack truck and dumped grace on me when He blessed me with your friendship, ladies.

Finally, my thanks to Maranatha Bible and Missionary Conference in Muskegon, Michigan, the real-life setting of Gilead Bible Conference. I grew up a short distance from the wood-framed Tabernacle, Prayer Tower, and stretch of shoreline that play a role in the setting of *Hallie's Heart*—places that imprinted my teen years with life-impacting memories. Later, as an adult, my life would be changed by Maranatha's writers' conference and the encouragement of Sandra Aldrich and Dick Bohrer. I am deeply grateful for Maranatha's ministry and its commitment to transforming lives for the glory of God.

Chapter One

Mona VanderMolen ran her fingers through her soggy red bangs for the fifth time in ten minutes. Her shoulders pulsated with a burning throb as she glanced at the cracked crystal of her Timex. Eleven twenty-five, and already the skin on her arms was glowing. *Another hour and I'll be crisp enough to serve up with a side of slaw and home fries.*

For the umpteenth time, she wished she could throttle Eskel Barkel. If he hadn't called and riled her up as she'd been flying out the shop door, she'd have remembered the sunscreen, golf umbrella, and frayed straw hat she always stashed in her aging F-150 on auction days. The hat, umbrella, and truck hadn't done much for her image since she'd moved to Stewartville. But then, Mona had never been much for image anyway. Especially when she was surrounded by cash croppers and dairy farmers waiting to see what outfit a city woman might be sporting as she tried to navigate around the occasional barnyard cow pie.

A lot of use the hat and sunscreen were now, crowning the clutter on her office desk. Clutter that Mona knew would hover over her thoughts all day like a fly on an outhouse door. Topping the stack was Eskel Barkel's laughable offer, on imposing legal letterhead, suggesting he buy out her shop. Beneath that was a scrawling, half-read note from Ellen, the heavy swooping flourishes almost shouting in anger. Then, billowing out from beneath her sister's note, was a pile of bills that Mona wasn't sure how she was going to pay. Bills were just one more thing to be unsure about these days. Piles of bills. Piles of uncertainties.

She swatted at a yellow jacket that had taken an interest in her flaming hair. One thing was certain. If she didn't get out of the sun soon, she was going to collapse from heatstroke right there between a wringer washer and a rosewood marimba. It would probably be the most exciting thing to happen in Stewartville in months. A sure-fire headliner for the "Comings and Goings" column of the *Stewartville Sentinel*. Mona was pretty sure a middle-aged woman collapsing from heatstroke could top the first "Comings and Goings" article she'd read in the paper over a bowl of chicken gumbo at Trina's Diner the day she'd moved to town: *Miss Esther Echams fell down her basement steps last Thursday. She was found by her sister, Miss Eula Echams, who called 9-1-1. No bones were broken, but Miss Esther was greatly discolored.* It was the moment Mona's heart told her that her move to Stewartville would change her life in ways defying explanation.

She surveyed the rows of unsold farm equipment spread across the back yard, stretching from the pristine white barn to the turn-of-the-century brick foursquare. The situation didn't look promising. Duane Meller had just finished auctioning the battered milkers that had been the lifeblood of the Bailey centennial farm. And his substantially built brother-in-law, Murel, whose job was to haul merchandise to the various pickups and minivans parked along the gravel road, was doing a pretty good job scarring up a lawn that had been mowed by Thurmond Bailey every other summer day for sixty-two years. Murel was older than dirt and had a bad heart. Everyone in Stewartville was waiting for the day he'd drop dead in his tracks at one of Duane's estate sales. He hadn't missed one of his brother-in-law's auctions in fifty-three years. A big part of Murel's job was holding up the merchandise for everyone to see and offering insightful comments, such as how much your wife would appreciate you if you brought her home this pressure cooker without a lid. Everyone agreed that Vanna White herself couldn't do a better job than Murel, especially with the hauling and loading—even if she did look better in heels.

Mona figured the junk boxes would most likely go next. They were stacked on long plank tables mounted on sawhorses and arranged in a half-dozen rows across the side yard. Assorted cartons cradled collections of warped Tupperware, hand-knit afghans, and scraps of life from the empty farmhouse, to be rifled through and hauled away by the highest bidder. Mona loved the junk boxes. On her very first buying trip eighteen months before, she'd hovered over the jumbled cartons like a child, poring over the hodgepodge collections, imagining the memories each object represented. It had shocked her to discover that families would sell off the mementos that had given shape to their lives, no matter how insignificant. The idea still troubled her after a year and a half of buying people's memories for a living.

Mona had already rummaged through the Bailey junk boxes and found nothing worth much for resale. She knew Duane always saved the household antiques to sell last, like the quartersawn oak sideboard standing inside the screened-in porch of the red brick house. Ginny Mae Francis had been looking for one just like it for six months, and heaven knew she was one person in Stewartville who didn't seem to care about haggling for the best price. She could afford to pay top dollar, and she made sure everybody knew it. Lucky for Mona. And if the big city dealers with their fat wallets would just cooperate and collapse from heatstroke before she did, she figured she might actually make the rent this month without dipping into the meager remains of her parents' modest inheritance once again. Just the thought of her father's piercing gaze should have been enough to send a chill through her bones. Mona smiled with the irony. It seemed her dad couldn't offer a comfort even as simple as that on a hot summer day.

Mona fanned herself with a wilted auction notice in an effort to coax the thick, humid air across her face. Her mossy green eyes narrowed against the glare of the sun as she watched a thin young woman with stringy hair and a faded yellow blouse sorting through a box of dog-eared and outdated books. Beside her, a baby dozed fitfully beneath the canopy of a rickety stroller.

Mona shaded her eyes from the sun's glare with the limp flyer as she watched the young mother select two children's books from the box on the ground. Glancing over her shoulder, the woman slid them into an adjacent box containing remnants of a set of Blue Willow china and a half-dozen Agatha Christie mysteries. Her eyes flickered across the faces of those standing closest to her, like a child cheating on her homework. Mona dropped her gaze to her auction flyer and pretended to be reading. She hoped no one else had seen. Everyone knew that Duane didn't allow people to switch items in the junk boxes. If Murel spotted her, he'd bless her out good.

A vague sense of embarrassment washed over Mona as she thought of the dozens of children's books still boxed away in the loft closet over the shop. All her favorite stories carefully selected for Hallie and Stacy's summer visits. Worn and torn, with an occasional ice-cream stain dotting the pages, now relegated to the darkness. She wondered what titles the mother in the yellow blouse had chosen for her child.

The midday sun bit into the nape of Mona's neck below her short-cropped curls. The heat was positively maddening. Obviously, Duane wasn't going to get to the antiques and furniture for at least another hour, and she silently debated whether it was worth the wait. She fanned a new rhythm with the limp auction circular and reached into the cavern of her leather shoulder bag for her water bottle. She tugged at the sports nozzle with her teeth and squirted the tepid liquid into her mouth, holding it there a few moments before swallowing. Then she shot a stream onto her blazing neck and closed her eyes as the water drizzled in a rivulet down the small of her back.

The pile of bills pulled at her thoughts once again as she calculated her markup on the sideboard. It certainly helped that Ginny Mae had come into the shop and described a piece exactly like this one that she wanted to purchase to display the Depression glass she'd inherited from her mother that spring. That Depression glass was an answer to Mona's prayers. Everyone in Stewartville knew that whatever Ginny Mae wanted, Ginny Mae got. Mona just had to find a way to get it for Ginny Mae first.

Mona scanned the clumps of bidders clustered around the farm grounds. *No sign of dealers in the crowd,* she noted. But that would simply be too good to be true. She couldn't remember an auction in more than a year where she hadn't been bidding against at least one big city dealer willing to fork over Saks Fifth Avenue prices. Dealers with buckets of money compared to hers, it always seemed. She was pretty sure she couldn't even afford a bucket at the moment. Not that she'd bought the shop to become rich. But she had planned for it to provide the basics of life, like food and water and an occasional box of Godiva chocolate.

Water. She sighed and in desperation squirted the dregs of her sports bottle over her head, closing her eyes as the warm droplets trickled down the nape of her neck. She tried to close her mind to the nagging realities. The letter from Eskel. The angry letter from Ellen. The bills.

Things hadn't exactly zipped along according to plan in the year-and-a-half since the shop had become hers. There *had* been a plan. It was just coming together more slowly than she'd expected. Of course, that hadn't surprised most of her friends, and especially Ellen, who could never be called a friend—just a sister. They'd all told her she was crazy to walk away from a tenured teaching position for absolutely no good reason and take the risk of going into business for herself. Didn't she know that small companies went under every day—companies run by people who actually knew what they were doing? And what chance did a middle-aged English teacher with absolutely no business experience have of coaxing a living out of a small-town antique shop? Her friends had been painfully honest.

Ellen had been downright scathing. "It's not like you're a two-income household, Mona. Are you insane? And just who do you think is going to bail you out if the business flops? It's sure not going to be Phil and me. I think we've had enough to deal with these past two years, thanks to you. You're forty-five years old. For heaven's sake, grow up!"

Grow up? At forty-five, Mona was still surprised her sister's anger could pierce her heart like a child's. The words always found their mark. No matter how she steeled herself against the pain, it managed to take her breath away and leave her numb. Two years before, the numbness had won, and Mona had left teaching.

Buying the antique shop had seemed like the perfect thing to do at the time, even when it hadn't made sense to anyone else. Except maybe Hallie. Of course, Mona couldn't be sure what Hallie thought. Ellen had barely let the two of them speak since the accident. But Mona had always chosen to believe that Hallie understood, because she, more than anyone, was numb with the shared pain.

Now, in the sweltering heat, with bills piled high and a checkbook balance magnetized to negative numbers, doubts hammered away at Mona's thoughts. She couldn't imagine what she would do if she were forced to consider Eskel Barkel's offer to buy her out. She'd poured her heart and soul into making the antique shop and small loft apartment her own. And she'd come to love her close-knit farming community, though it still could be jarring to know that the fifteen hundred residents of Stewartville sometimes knew her business before she knew it herself.

Mona's midlife career change hadn't come without a price, and there were still days when she felt torn about the life she'd abandoned. Football games in the crisp fall air. Homecoming frenzy. Fanning a love for learning into a glowing ember in the hearts of her students. Not a day passed that she didn't think of the students.

More than anything, she missed her beautiful Lake Michigan beach house. It was her home in a way that the loft apartment could never be. The smells, the sounds, the serenity, and the savagery of the Big Lake were etched into her heart. Her most precious possessions were memories of the beach house, of Hallie and Stacy, and of the summers she had spent taking care of her nieces. She missed them more than she had believed possible.

Mona raked her fingers through her damp hair and forced her thoughts back to the auction. Yellow Blouse's box was next, and she clutched her bidding number in her left hand while her right gently rocked the stroller. Mona scanned the box. The children's books had most likely been slid to the bottom of the box, out of sight.

Mona's interest was drawn to the other bidders. The competition. Most were men she recognized from town, church, or other auctions, with the exception of a lanky man in crisp khaki Dockers and a chambray shirt, who appeared to be annoyingly comfortable in the heat. *Most likely a dealer,* she told herself, wondering why she hadn't noticed him earlier. Stewartville men came mostly from Scotch and German stock and were known more for sturdiness than stature. This man was one of the few in the crowd who could lay claim to a height of six feet or more and wasn't dressed in some form of denim and a baseball cap. His eyes were hidden behind narrow sunglasses that hugged his sandy, short-cropped hair. One corner of his mouth was drawn down in a smirk or a smile—Mona couldn't decide which. For a moment, she thought he might be staring at her, flaunting his private swath of shade beneath an enormous green-and-white-striped golf umbrella. Exactly the size and colors of her own umbrella, still leaning in the corner of her office. It was the ultimate offense.

Mona steamed silently, and her eyebrows arched in a silent challenge. For a moment she thought a smile flickered across his face as he dipped his umbrella in her direction, like a gentleman tipping his hat. Then he turned to watch Duane.

Mona wiped beads of sweat from her upper lip. *Great. Now I've ticked off a dealer with big bucks and a bigger attitude. Please, God, don't let him want my sideboard!* She stole another glance in the man's direction, but the dark glasses were turned toward the next item up for bid.

Duane Meller had moved to the junk boxes and was opening at a buck. Murel held a Blue Willow serving bowl and saucer high over his head so the crowd could see the two most saleable items in the box. Yellow Blouse's bidding number flashed into the air. Thirty-one.

"Do I have a dollah fifty? Who'll give a dollah, fifty and a dollah? Dollah, dollah, fifty and a dollah?"

Mona knew she could bid the box up and still make a profit on the half-dozen dinner and luncheon plates. Blue Willow was always popular. But not today. Today the box would be her secret gift to Yellow Blouse.

"Sold, to number thirty-one for a measly dollah. You got the bargain of the day, honey. A lotta readin' in that box. Murel, help the lady get that thing loaded in her car so's she don't have to drag it off herself."

Murel. *How does he manage to haul plunder like a pack mule in this heat?* Mona mused. In bibs and work boots, no less. Some people were a wonder, and it seemed to Mona that a good many of them lived in Stewartville.

Her thoughts shifted to the half-read letter from Ellen that lay on her office desk. One could depend on Ellen to write letters when she wanted to avoid conversation. She always avoided people who had the audacity to disagree with her. Without opening it, Mona knew what the letter would say. A rehash of their phone conversation days before when she'd begged Ellen to let Hallie spend a few weeks with her over the summer. This time, Mona had tried to make the appeal logical, rational, and totally unemotional. It would be great to have a fifteen-year-old help out in the shop and go on buying trips. Hallie could help her set up the new office and organize her files. Elsie could use the break and spend a little time with her grandkids. And Ellen and Phil could schedule a getaway to the Caymans or perhaps Aruba.

Mona had promised to keep an eye on Hallie every minute. Every second of every minute. She'd even thought about adding a PS to her letter: *There are no bodies of water within fifteen miles of Stewartville. Hallie will be safe.* Of course, she never could have actually written such a thing, but she'd toyed with the idea until a gentle conviction settled over her soul and redirected her heart.

Mona knew the letter held another cold, edgy no. The same answer she'd heard again and again. The same tone. The same silent, screaming accusation.

"And now, ladies and gents, we're moving on to the antiques on the front porch and the other furniture in the house to get a little break from this sun. Not a lotta air in the house, but at least a little shade. If you'll just follow me."

A murmur of appreciation rippled through the assembled bidders as Duane Meller turned toward the brick farmhouse. Slowly, he removed his wide-brimmed straw hat and mopped his bald forehead with a faded blue bandanna pulled from the back pocket of his boot-cut Levi's as he walked. Elda Ann, his wife of fifty-three years, and auction assistant for just as many, followed him. She pushed the creaking, wheeled metal podium she'd used to record bids for as long as Meller Auction Service had been in existence.

The crowd languidly abandoned their positions among the scattered equipment on the front lawn and straggled along behind Duane. Yellow Blouse shrugged her shoulders, then turned the stroller down the gravel driveway toward a rusty gray Cutlass leaning into the drainage ditch along the dirt road. In her peripheral vision, Mona could see the tall man collapsing his umbrella. His head was turned in her direction, and the crooked grin still pulled at the corners of his mouth. Mona looked away and wished for a few more drops of water in her sports bottle to squirt at his smug face. She ran a few paces to catch up to Duane and get a good spot inside the house.

Certainly Ellen would say okay this time. She couldn't expect to keep Hallie away forever. But the moment the thought came to Mona, she knew it was a lie. It was *exactly* what Ellen expected to do.

A familiar uneasiness gripped Mona's heart as she remembered the empty look in Hallie's eyes the last time she'd seen her. Phil and Ellen had brought her to the grand opening of the shop more than a year ago, then had managed to make apologies and slip Hallie away before Mona had found a moment to draw her niece aside and ask her how she *really* was.

But Hallie's eyes had said it all. The pain was consuming her. She was slipping away.

The bidding was ready to begin, and Mona knew what she had to do. She would call that afternoon, and this time she would make Ellen understand. She would force her to say yes to just one long weekend.

She prayed Ellen would listen, just this once.

Chapter Two

Hallie couldn't believe she'd been stupid enough to forget to check the gas before she'd pulled out of the driveway, but it wasn't like she'd ever planned a 2 AM getaway before. She knew she was an idiot to pull into a truck stop alone in the middle of the night, but what choice did she have? *Just get in and get out, girl,* she told herself.

She didn't even consider taking off her helmet or her father's oversized leather jacket as she swung her bike into a bay facing the exit. When she'd left the house, she'd carefully tucked her unruly, waist-length red curls into a bandanna before slipping on her helmet.

Now, at the worst possible moment, the scarf betrayed her.

Under the pressure of her thick mass of curls, it had unknotted, and several strands had escaped down her back. In the seconds it took to pump her gas, she realized her attempts to look like another guy on a bike were in the Dumpster. Still, she had enough sense not to add a drive-off to her list of Crimes of the Day.

She dashed into the truck stop and slapped ten bucks on the abandoned counter, but as she wheeled to leave, she saw she wasn't alone. Her path was blocked by a wiry man not much taller than she was, in worn jeans and an orange T-shirt, with a faded blue dragon tattoo covering his right forearm.

"Well, what do we have here? A little red-headed biker chick out cruisin' in the middle of the night. And it looks to me like you're all by yourself. Now isn't that just a dirty shame."

Even through the face shield, Hallie caught a whiff of alcohol.

If a cashier was present in the building, they weren't making an appearance. Behind Hallie, in the truckers' lounge at the end of a long hall, a television blared. She took a small step backward as panic began to rise in her chest.

Don't go that way, something whispered inside her. *Go for the door.*

She slipped her hand beneath her chaps, into her jeans pocket, and wrapped her fingers around the small canister of mace she'd taken from a kitchen drawer before she'd left. She prayed it would work.

She eased to the right and calculated the shortest route to the door, between the racks of sunflower seeds, beef jerky, and assorted chips. She figured if she hadn't already used up all her luck for the night, Mr. Blue Dragon Tattoo would be too drunk to stop her.

Instead, the man mirrored her movements and took a step toward her.

"No need to be hurryin' off, little lady. What you got hidin' under all that leather?"

He grabbed at her arm, and Hallie jerked it away as she shifted the mace into position deep within her pocket, nozzle pointing forward. Her ignition key was still clutched in her right hand.

"Touch me again and you'll regret it, you creep."

The man edged closer, and Hallie saw his eyes flicker across the store. No cashier. No customers pulling in. Truckers in the back either watching TV or asleep. His eyes darted back.

In one fluid move, he grabbed Hallie, spun her into a headlock, and dragged her toward the door.

His strength shocked her. In a moment, they'd be in the parking lot, and the doors of the truck stop would swing closed behind them.

Hallie writhed and tried to scream, but the man's grip on her neck tightened, cutting off her air. He paused for a split-second to swing open one side of the double-glass doors to the parking lot, and she took her chance, slamming the heel of her black boot onto the toes of filthy tennis shoes. With her right hand she plunged her motorcycle key into the faded tattoo and twisted.

The man grunted and loosened his hold for one fleeting instant. Hallie whirled and delivered a stream of mace into his contorted face, sending a blast directly into his gaping mouth. Then she turned and ran for her life.

His screams and curses followed her as she tore across the parking lot, jumped on her Fat Boy, and hit the starter button. "Thank God for electronic ignition," she whispered to herself.

Throwing a final, panicked glance over her shoulder, she gripped the throttle so tightly that she sprayed a cloud of gravel behind the Harley like a stuntwoman in a biker movie. Careening out of the parking lot at a speed that would have made her parents collapse in horror, her dirt-riding experience paid off as she sped across an open field, onto the entrance ramp, and back onto

I-96, heading northwest away from Grand Rapids.

For the next half hour, Hallie checked her rearview mirror every few seconds, expecting to see a semi barreling after her. Her hands were cramping and her shoulders knotting. She pulled her left hand away from the clutch, slapped it on her black leather chaps, and flexed her fingers until pinpricks swelled in her palm.

"Stupid, stupid, stupid!"

Her words were drowned out by the pummeling gusts that whipped around the windshield as she tore through the night.

Dear God, that pervert could have killed me and no one would've ever known. I hope I broke every bone in his foot!

Her imagination replayed the scene, lingering for a moment on the horrific ending she'd somehow managed to escape. Panic tightened her throat as she struggled to focus on the halo of her headlight on the desolate interstate.

You're fine now. He was just a stupid drunk. Don't think about it.

Another body-jolting gust of warm June air hammered at her shoulders. She could barely remember the thirty miles she had traveled since fleeing the truck stop. As she raced along, her eyes searched the wooded median for signs of a police cruiser.

A bit ironic, Hallie told herself. Only hours before, she'd done everything possible to avoid being noticed by the police. She was pretty certain they'd have an opinion about her stealing her father's motorcycle in the middle of the night. Not to mention that she wasn't a licensed driver. She'd knocked the wind out of her parents with her stunts the past couple of years, but landing in jail would certainly raise the bar.

The way she figured, it would be at least twelve hours before they'd notice she'd taken the bike and run away. Then it would be another two or three while they argued about what to do. Her mother would be too embarrassed to call the cops. And her dad would be half furious, half proud that his little Hal actually had the guts to take off on one of his precious bikes.

She'd spent days figuring angles and planning details. Complications had never been part of the plan. Especially complications involving a drunk, angry trucker looking to finish what she couldn't even make herself think he'd tried to start. "I don't think so," she muttered as she cranked the throttle. The acceleration drove her back into her seat.

She couldn't remember the last time she'd driven a motorcycle after dark. Her mother never allowed it, and it was one of the few rules Dad ever backed her up on. His opinions on anything were few and far between these days, except for the ones he screamed at her mother behind closed doors. But he'd stuck to his guns and had rarely let Hal on the bike after dark, even in the yard.

And he'd lectured Hallie about safe driving. Over and over again. It was no secret that EMTs had scraped him off the pavement a few times in his life.

"The speed limit's not a suggestion for teenagers, Hallie. Wait until you're old enough to know what you're doing before you decide to take your life in your hands. Someday, when you're my age, you'll realize that most rules are optional, especially the ones that get you where you want to go."

It hadn't made a lot sense to Hallie the day he'd said it. A day when she was twelve and they were flying down Woodward Avenue doing seventy-seven with the top down on the Corvette. But in the months after Stacy died, his words seemed to explain a lot. *"Someday you'll realize that most rules are optional, except the ones that get you where you want to go."* Rules such as, do what's right for yourself, in spite of what anybody else thinks. If anger works, be angry. If silence works, be silent. If money helps you forget, work eighty hours a week. Buy lots of toys to flaunt in front of anybody willing to be impressed. Show them your four Harleys and your Corvette, and maybe they'll forget that your daughter's not nearly as impressive as your stuff.

She glanced at the speedometer. Eighty-three.

Slow down, Hal. Wipe out at this speed, and they'll have to identify you with dental records.

She willed her fingers to ease back until the bike slowed and the drone of the engine dropped to a lower, more familiar thrum. Eighty miles an hour on a dark Michigan highway was attempted suicide. One deer, one pothole, one seam in the pavement, and she'd never see her sixteenth birthday. She wasn't quite ready for that.

The thought of death washed over her with a familiar, stunning force. In the past two years, it had insinuated itself into every fiber of her life, hovering on the fringes of every waking moment and stalking her nightmares in the suffocating stillness of the night.

The nights were the worst. She had decided it would be the most frightening thing about breaking into Aunt Mona's house. She would be totally alone at night for the first time in two years.

The idea was a jumble of terror and irresistible attraction, like the way she felt when the seatbelt tightened on her first roller coaster ride. Six months ago, even the thought of it would have been impossible. But that was before she'd found the picture.

She'd been flipping through a travel magazine, searching for scenes to scan into a history project, when the photo jumped off the page. A Michigan lighthouse, the beacon at Pere Marquette Park, silhouetted against an orange sunset. In a heartbeat, she was breathless, as if something had sucked the air from her lungs and left her for dead. For what seemed an eternity, her gaze had lingered on the page in the silence of her father's study. Then she had gently folded the magazine and slipped it back into place on the cherry bookshelf.

She'd seen that lighthouse hundreds of times before. She knew the cadence of the surf breaking on the nearby beach in the summer. And she knew the power of the current within the arms of the breakwater, one moment caressing your legs, the next moment sucking you beneath the surface and dragging you like a rag doll until your lungs were crushed. She knew the sight of a lifeless body being dragged to shore, followed by screams unrecognizable as her own.

Over the next few days, the cadence of the waves had echoed in Hallie's heart, overwhelming her with a roar of memories that threatened to pull her, too, beneath the surface. With the deafening rhythm, a growing certainty had gripped her. So she had stolen her father's motorcycle and the wad of cash her mother kept hidden in her jewelry armoire, and set out to face the demons of her past or die trying. She had not yet decided whether to face death or embrace it. She only knew that she was already dying—and she wasn't sure she cared.

Hallie's eyes were drawn to the rearview mirror again and again, checking for approaching headlights as the miles slipped away. Nothing. Another ten miles and she'd be there. She glanced uneasily toward the horizon, trying to gauge the lifespan of the darkness. She prayed the dawn would hold back long enough for her to reach the cottage under cover of dark.

The green sign for her exit appeared in the distance. She pulled in the clutch and coasted down an incline and around a gentle bend to the west. Airline Road was next. She would finally be off the interstate and one step closer to safety. Her hands were still cramping and her shoulders were knotting, so she forced her thoughts elsewhere, anywhere, back home to the day she'd decided to leave.

She'd made up her mind the night her mother waved brochures for camps for troubled kids under her nose. Hallie still remembered the words she'd spat into her mother's face: "Sign up for a camp for screwed-up parents first, and get back to me." She almost regretted the look of horror that had appeared on her mother's face.

For a moment, Hallie imagined what it would be like when her parents got home and found the note she'd left on their bed. Her mother would totally freak, and her father would go dead silent. They'd probably call Aunt Mona first, but Aunt Mona wouldn't know where she was. Then Mom would go totally ballistic and scream a lot about how could Hallie do such a thing to her; then maybe she'd give her shrink a call.

Aunt Mona would offer to drive down from Stewartville, and Mom would refuse to let her come. Hallie had always been able to count on Aunt Mona, and her mom hated them both for it.

Aunt Mona would tell her mother that she would pray. It was what Aunt Mona always did. The kind of prayers that made you feel like God was right next to you. The kind of prayers she'd prayed with Hallie and Stacy snuggled close in the loft of the beach house at sunset. Mom would hate her for that, too.

Hallie suddenly felt exhausted. Her arms ached, and her legs cried out to be stretched straight. She envisioned the yellow gingham coverlet, over-stuffed lace pillow shams, and creamy white walls of Aunt Mona's guest room. The room where her mother and father typically stayed for a polite twenty-four hours before leaving Hallie and Stacy for their yearly summer flings with Aunt Mona.

Her body ached for sleep, but she knew that sleep would be the hardest part of all this. To sleep in the guest room with the loft overshadowing her. Or maybe even to sleep at all.

The sign for Hoffmaster State Park appeared on the left as Hallie cruised the curves on the shore-line road. *Just another half mile to the turnoff into the subdivision, and then the lane to the cottage,* she reminded herself.

As she neared the entrance to the subdivision, she accelerated as much as she dared and then cut the engine, leaning into the left-hand turn in the direction of the dunes. The bike coasted silently past the homes at the foot of the enormous sand ridge separating the shoreline road from the beach. As the road curved to the right, the bike slowed, and Hallie turned the Harley down a narrow paved lane running between two ranch houses. In the moonlight, the path was almost indiscernible. It was the spot that had always meant she was finally *there,* at Aunt Mona's house. She drifted silently up the dune and down the right-hand fork where the gravel driveway began. The bike came to a stop just six feet from the barnwood shed.

Hallie eased the bike onto its kickstand. She knew if it tipped, it would take three of her to set it upright again. Other than the residents who owned the stretch of private beach, few people knew the lane existed. Aunt Mona's was the only house along the lane between the subdivision and the lake. People walking the lane to the beach could pass right by and not know they'd missed it. Trees surrounded the house on every side except in front, which gave way to a stunning view of Lake Michigan. A view Hallie hadn't seen in two years.

She stooped and picked up a fake plastic rock to the right of the shed door. Popping open a hidden compartment in the rock, she withdrew a key and inserted it in the padlock. The double doors opened easily, swinging on hinges that creaked loudly in the darkness. Setting her helmet carefully in the sand, Hallie drew a Maglite from her leather saddlebag and twisted on the beam. The shed was just as she'd remembered it. A half-dozen beach chairs hung in evenly spaced rows on studs where the walls met the slope of the roof. Below them, rakes, brooms, hoses, and a few garden tools hung on pegs and hooks. In the right-hand corner stood Aunt Mona's cherished cherry-wood tool chest that had belonged to Grandpa VanderMolen.

Hallie pulled off her gloves and zipped them into her jacket pocket. She retrieved her helmet and stepped inside the shed, the toe of her boot brushing up against a black plastic garbage can that claimed most of the floor space. She pulled the garbage can out and around to the back of the shed where it would be invisible to anyone approaching the house from the driveway. Behind the shed, the dune rose slightly to a path leading through the woods to the condos farther down the beach. She scanned the dune and the path, then returned to the shed to look for the house key.

Aunt Mona kept the house key inside a metal medicine cabinet nailed to the back wall of the shed. Hallie found it within seconds, slid it into her pocket, and went back outside to drag in the Harley.

The first pale washes of daylight were peeking

through the trees as she heaved the six-hundred-pound motorcycle over the threshold and into the shed, secured it on its kickstand, and quickly emptied the soft leather saddlebags on either side. Then she carefully draped the bike with a green and orange floral bedsheet she found hanging on a nail. It seemed silly to care about dust collecting on her dad's bike in light of everything else she'd done with it, but she did it anyway. Then she eased the squeaky shed doors closed and snapped the padlock, tucking the key into her pocket as she gathered her bags and turned toward the house.

Every detail of the beach house reflected Aunt Mona's love for the turn-of-the-century structure. A white wraparound porch embraced pale yellow clapboard on all but the rear side. Hallie stepped onto the south arm of the porch that ran the full length of the house. The familiar antique oak pew still rested between the welcoming windows. She paused for a moment and took a long, slow breath before rounding the corner to catch her first glimpse of the water.

The softly pulsating waves glimmered in the early morning light in a widening golden ribbon that stretched from the beach sand to the horizon. For a moment, her breathing stopped.

Memories flashed in her mind as if a mob of paparazzi had suddenly invaded her brain. Aunt Mona climbing quietly into the loft and nudging two sleeping girls awake just before pale pink swaths painted the sky. The three of them sitting on the porch steps with chocolate-covered dough-nuts and milk, watching the early dawn light shimmer on the water. Late summer outings to pick blueberries.

Hallie crumpled to the slatted porch as her legs gave way beneath her. She pressed her back against the cool clapboard siding of the house and drew her knees to her chin, her breath now coming in quiet moans. She was unaware of how long she sat, her arms wrapped around her knees, rocking gently and grieving.

Stacy is dead.

Nothing can bring her back.

Stacy is dead.

No-o-o-o.

The sobs rose from a place so deep within her heart that she felt they would rip her in two. The cadence of the waves pulsated, rising and falling with Hallie's gasping breath, gently stroking her wounded heart.

With time, her weeping subsided, and the hard, familiar truth knotted itself in her chest again. She sat until the sound of the waves was all she could hear, until the rending of her heart had slipped back into numbness.

Slowly, she gathered her scattered belongings and slid the house key from her pocket. It was time to go in.

In that same instant, she realized she wasn't

alone. Someone had been watching from the bushes near the house.

A scream rose in her throat as she saw that it was a man.

Chapter Three

Mona was starved. She reached across the truck seat, grabbed her cavernous leather purse, and fished for a bag of peanut M&M's. Her knee steadied the bulky box truck as it headed north over the rolling hills of M-66.

What a waste of time, she fumed. *Standing for six hours in the scorching sun for a couple of trunks, a copper boiler, and a pressed-back rocker. Just so I could end my day watching the Sweatless Wonder drive off with my furniture.*

She had dropped out of the bidding at $275. The khaki-clad dealer had walked away with Ginny Mae's sideboard for $285. In a final humiliation, he'd flashed a devastating smile in her direction as he loaded the piece into his freshly waxed Suburban. Mona had pretended not to see him as she slowly squeezed her truck between his vehicle and an adjacent minivan to make the quickest possible escape. Sticking out her tongue would have felt better. Especially when she saw him heft the massive piece of furniture in a single motion. It didn't help that her hair was sodden, her skin scorched, and her face dripping with sweat.

Chocolate would help. It always helped.

Mona surveyed her face in the rearview mirror as she headed back to Stewartville. Her fair complexion made her susceptible to heat, and after six hours in the sun, her skin shone tomato red. The tight, burning pain on her shoulders reminded her how stupid she had been to wear a sleeveless blouse on a scorching June day. Most of the farms in central Michigan didn't boast much in the way of shade trees. She wondered if by the time the burn healed she'd have thrown in the towel and sold the shop to Eskel Barkel.

It always came back to money, and Mona never seemed to have enough. She dreaded facing Elsie's questions about why she'd come back with next to no purchases. Elsie would be certain that if *she* had been with Mona at the auction, they would have come home with the entire estate without spending more than twenty bucks. Then she'd most likely spend the rest of her day informing the few customers that might come through the door that they should all pray, Lord willing, that Mona would eventually get the hang of the auction business before the shop went belly-up.

Mona's fingers found the lumpy package at the bottom of her purse. She ripped it open with her teeth and poured a dozen half-melted blobs into her mouth. She certainly deserved a treat after the morning she'd had, and she knew the perfect thing—a crispy chicken salad drizzled with sweet-and-sour dressing from Trina's Café, and a huge glass of raspberry iced tea. After she'd run over for takeout, she'd unload the truck and give Harold a chance to look over the day's purchases.

She made an easy right onto County Road 13 and popped a few more M&M's into her mouth. It hadn't been easy boosting the trunks into the back of the truck. But years of jogging on Lake Michigan beach sand had made her five-foot-ten-inch frame lean and muscular, and she wasn't about to ask Murel to lug her purchases for her. She'd learned that a single woman needed to work for respect in a farming community, and she'd never been afraid of work.

Over the next crest to the east lay Stewartville and home. Home. It seemed an awkward word. Three years ago, she'd never dreamed that home would be a loft above her own antique shop in a tiny farming town. Just eight years away from a comfortable retirement, she'd walked away from a career as an English teacher at West Shore High School. Everyone had told her she was nuts, and they were probably right. Almost everyone asked why, but Mona's answers were always vague. A few friends reminded her that she didn't have a husband—as if, perhaps, she'd never noticed.

Most of her close friends knew it wasn't a decision about teaching. The drowning had changed everything in Mona's world. Within days of the funeral, she had known she had to leave the beach house for a while, to find another place to heal. She'd refused to sell, though, knowing that her home would someday find its way back into her life. She didn't doubt that the time would come. The only question was when.

So much had changed. Ellen had nearly disowned her after Stacy's death. The pain of losing Hallie, too, had torn at Mona's heart with a grief that sucked the life from her. She'd had nothing left for her students, and her passion for teaching had withered. She'd submitted her resignation quietly and quickly, made plans to close up the house, and then waited and prayed.

Within days, three to be exact, Cousin Elsie had called to inquire about whether Mona would be interested in buying out her friend Harold's interest in the Stewartville Antique Shop. Harold's doctors had recommended semi-retirement at the ripe old age of seventy-six, and he was looking for someone to learn the business but who would still let him putter in the workroom. And not to worry, Elsie would continue running the day-to-day operation of the store, just as she had for Harold for the past seventeen years.

As a child, Mona had been moderately frightened of her eccentric cousin Elsie, who was given to speaking her mind to anyone about anything and who wore clothing reminiscent of a deranged gypsy. Community gossip held that when Elsie

McFeeney stood on her front porch to call her grandkids in for dinner, folks could hear her a mile away. Mona had never had any reason to believe they were exaggerating.

Thirty years Mona's elder, Elsie had always stirred a sense of awe in her. She lived in a world of black and white, where answers were clear-cut and doled out to friends and family in hearty proportions. It seemed to Elsie's way of thinking that Mona was the answer to Harold's dilemma and Harold was the answer to Mona's, and it would be good if Mona could get him an answer by the end of the week. Just like that. A year-and-a-half later, Mona still wasn't sure why she'd said yes. But she'd called Nathan McDaniel, who had handled her finances for years, and asked him to make the arrangements from her parents' inheritance account.

A garish orange water tower rose on the horizon, and Mona slowed her speed to thirty-five. Stewartville's speed trap was a dependable source of revenue for the town. Mona had learned that lesson the hard way. She was pretty sure Officer Spencer probably had her driver's license memorized by now.

On the north side of Main, McNally's Feed Store and the stone-fronted Crystal Flash gas station occupied the first block, followed by four blocks of storefronts owned by folks who all seemed to have sprung from the same sturdy family tree. Miller's IGA, Peterson's Auto Repair, Trina's Café, and the Curl Up and Dye Hair Salon. On the south side, a new mini McDonalds offered the town's only real fast food, unless you counted the Dairy Delight further down the street, where every baseball team in town gathered after their games. The south side of the street also boasted the new, colonial-style First Federal Bank and a six-lane bowling alley with newly installed, computerized scoring just like the city lanes in Grand Rapids. Dawson's Drugs anchored the east end of the business district, along with a small parking lot adjacent to the pharmacy that had been cordoned off for resurfacing for the past two weeks.

Mona turned north a block before Stewartville's only traffic light, then east again down a gravel alley that flanked the north side Main Street businesses. Near the end of the block, she pulled the F-150 off to the side, near doors marked "Stewartville Antiques, Deliveries Only." Harold could back the thing up, and they'd unload it later, she decided, after that raspberry tea and salad.

Mona crammed the last handful of M&M's into her mouth, grabbed her purse, and headed into the shop through a green door on the left side of the building. The smell of paint thinner and polyurethane confirmed that Harold had been at work. His latest project, a walnut highboy, stood on a paint- and stain-splotched tarp on the left side of the room. The deep tones of the wood shone on the door fronts where the paint had been removed.

Mona glanced around the crowded, high-ceilinged workroom, but Harold was nowhere to be seen. Furniture waiting to be refinished was stacked in rows along the rough brick walls. A twelve-foot workbench ran the full length of the north wall, and white painted pegboard hung above it with a profusion of tools displayed in orderly rows categorized by function. The man was a stickler for order.

Mona hoped he hadn't finally succumbed to the fumes. A day seldom passed when she didn't throw open the heavy delivery doors and chide Harold about proper ventilation. He'd listen and nod politely, then wait for Mona to leave before he closed the doors again. Despite his stubbornness, Harold Rawlings ranked high on Mona's list of blessings. He practically lived at the shop, despite their arrangement that he would provide part-time help. He was meticulous to a fault, working as a handyman, refinisher, appraiser, and consultant. His love for antiques bordered on passion, and his knowledge and expertise were irreplaceable.

"That you, Mona?" a voice shrilled from the front of the shop.

"Yes, Elsie, I'm back." Mona made a mental note, not for the first time, to check her insurance policy for details regarding breakage of crystal and china.

"Well, how'd you make out in this infernal heat? I'll be just a minute, dear. This window display is all wrong, and I thought a little rearrangement might give it a boost. I *don't* believe the blue gingham tablecloth is quite right for this display of Fiesta ware, so I brought along something from home this morning."

Mona pushed through the café doors separating the shop from the workroom and tossed her purse onto an oak swivel chair in the small office Harold had just finished framing last week. Before Mona had bought the shop, Harold had operated his office from the workroom, but Mona had claimed the loft as her home and created an office in a corner of the showroom.

Elsie's voice was coming from the display window at the front of the store, where two feet in tiny, hot-pink Keds protruded from beneath a floral chintz curtain that served as a backdrop.

"I'm sure it will be quite lovely when you're finished, Elsie. Has anyone been in today?"

Mona plopped onto a maroon horsehair settee and glanced around for something to fan herself with. The pink shoes beneath the curtain wobbled a bit, and she heard the *chink* of one piece of pottery against another. She winced.

"Need any help in there?"

Mona had searched for hours Saturday evening after the shop closed, looking for a yellow gingham tablecloth for the Fiesta ware display.

But like most things or people she came into contact with, Elsie had obviously decided the display could be improved upon.

"Not a bit, my dear. I have it all under control."

Mona fought the urge to roll her eyes. The chintz curtains billowed and then settled again as the tiny, bright shoes disappeared.

"Sharon Wendel did come in this morning looking for copper boilers to use for storin' all those magazine she likes to hoard. I believe she is one young lady who should be encouraged to get a grip on her household clutter. I told her that as soon as you picked one up, you'd set it aside for her. I don't suppose you got one today?"

Mona brightened. "Well, as a matter of fact, I did." She found a wrinkled take-out menu from Trina's at the bottom of her purse and fanned herself vigorously.

The chintz curtains heaved aside, and Elsie emerged. She was a short, wiry woman with barely a hundred pounds on her tiny frame, but her hands were surprisingly large and punctuated by hot pink fingernails. Her hair resembled a cloud of lavender cotton candy and was fluffed into a soft bun. Several wisps had fallen loose at the nape and curled into soft tendrils. Deep crow's-feet radiated from her pale blue eyes, and her mouth was highlighted with the most recent lipstick featured at the Curl Up and Dye Hair Salon, Passion Plum. She wore flaming pink polyester slacks, a baby blue cotton blouse, and a cobbler's apron in floral pastels with pink piping.

"My heavens, child, you *do* look like your face is about to explode. I suppose you didn't take enough water to drink. You know there isn't a lick of shade at the Bailey farm. I imagine we'd just better get a fan on you and cool you off."

She took Mona by the arm and commandeered her back through the shop to the small, unfinished office, which smelled of pine studs. Mona had to admit she felt more than a little warm, and a cool drink sounded heavenly. Elsie threw Mona's purse to the floor, pushed her gently into the chair, and returned to the showroom to find one of several tall, oscillating floor fans.

"I don't suppose you had any lunch either?" Elsie hollered over the sound of metal feet scraping against the wooden floor. She stated it like an indictment of Mona's character.

"Not really."

"Not really? Meaning you sucked down some M&M's, I suppose."

Elsie was muttering under her breath as she dragged the fan through the office door and plugged it in. She disappeared into the workroom, emerging a moment later with a Styrofoam box and a tall, lidded paper cup.

"Now eat. It's crispy chicken salad with sweet-and-sour dressing and raspberry iced tea from

Trina's." She shoved the box and the cup into Mona's hands.

Mona stared at the lunch for a moment, and then burst into laughter.

"Well, for heaven's sake," Elsie sputtered, placing her hands on her hips. "Try to do a favor for people and they laugh at you." Mona winced inwardly, her eyes searching Elsie's face for any shadow of hurt.

"No, no, it's the most wonderful thing anyone could have done for me, Elsie. That's why I'm laughing. It's exactly what I needed, and I didn't even have to tell you. You amaze me, that's all. Thank you." Mona reached out and gently stroked Elsie's arm.

"Well then."

Mona had long ago learned to recognize Elsie's version of *thank you,* and she watched as her cousin busied herself picking imaginary lint from her cobbler's apron.

Mona broke the brief silence as she popped open the lid on the salad. "So, no business today except for Sharon Wendel?" She unwrapped the plastic silverware and stabbed a straw into her drink. Elsie leaned against the door frame, her arms crossed against her chest.

"Some lookers. You know, just window-shoppin' for something to do. And Ginny Mae did come in and look around for a while. Shoulda put her to work organizin' those files you got piled in your office. I sure haven't lived to be my age to be alphabetizin' like some fresh-faced secretary. That girl's got too much time on her hands for her own good! Needs to learn which end of a broom's the one you sweep with. You did get a couple of calls, though. A man. Sounded kinda young, wouldn't tell me what he wanted. Said he'd call back and talk to you. Pretty fishy, if you ask me."

"Really? Did he give you any idea what it was about? You know, I'm waiting to hear from Elmer Dean about what time to show up tomorrow to look over his reproductions. But since he's pushing seventy-five, we can probably rule him out, unless he's on some new kinda vitamin."

The phone rang as Mona was attacking her first bite of salad. Munching furiously, she waved at Elsie to answer it. Swooping down, Elsie plucked up a cordless from a corner of the office.

"Stewartville Antique Shop. Elsie McFeeney speaking. Yes, she's right here. Might take an extra second for her to swallow that big mouthful she's workin' on, but, here she is."

Mona grabbed the receiver and scowled in Elsie's direction. The voice on the other end was babbling hysterically.

"Mona, Hallie's missing! Is she with you? Let me talk to her right this instant!"

Mona froze, then slowly lowered her fork.

"Ellen, what's going on? She's not with me. I haven't spoken to her in weeks. You know that."

"No, I *don't* know that. Phil and I came back this afternoon from an overnight to Stratford and found a note. There's not a word in it about where she's gone or when she'll be back. And Phil's Fat Boy is missing. She's run away! I can't believe she'd do something like this to us."

Mona was dumbstruck. She knew Hallie had been struggling with depression and nightmares, and Ellen and Phil had been at their wits' end trying to help her. But she'd never imagined that Hallie would do anything like this.

"What about her friends?"

"Not a word."

"Her boyfriend? Jason, wasn't it? He'd certainly know."

"He doesn't have a clue. They haven't been on the best of terms lately, anyway. If she's with you, Mona, you have to tell us. You can't hide her from us."

Mona could hear the desperation in her sister's voice. Something like this could push Ellen over the edge. She'd always been high-strung, and Stacy's death had almost killed her.

"Don't be ridiculous, Ellen, of course I'd tell you. I'd never condone Hallie putting you through something like this. Look, I'm going to throw a few things in a bag and come down there. I can be in Bloomfield Hills in three hours."

"Oh, please, Mona, would you?" Ellen sobbed. "You're the only one she's ever listened to. I should have agreed to let her come see you this summer, but I couldn't stand the idea of having her gone. It terrifies me. And things have been so ugly between us . . . between Hallie and me . . . between you and me—"

"Stop that right now," Mona said, cutting her off mid-sentence. "We've had hard times, but there are no hard feelings between us, at least as far as I'm concerned. We're family, and if you hadn't called me, it would have broken my heart."

There was silence for a moment and quiet sobbing at the other end of the line.

"I can't lose both of them, Mona. I'll die."

"You're not going to lose Hallie, Ellen. She just needed to get away. She left a note for you and Phil to find. She'll probably call you before I get there. Now I need to talk to Elsie about covering a few things for me before I leave, so I need to go. Is Phil there with you?"

"Yes."

"Good. It's going to be okay, Ellen. God knows where she is, and He's watching over her."

"Right." The tone had chilled once more to ice. "I hope not the same way He watched over Stacy. I think this family's had more than enough of *His* help." Silence fell again, punctuated with sobs.

"I need to go, Mona. There's a police officer at the door." With a click, Ellen was gone.

Elsie had reappeared in the doorway with a steno pad and pen.

"Just tell me what you need, honey."

Mona rested her head in her hands and tried to gather her thoughts.

"I need you to call Elmer and tell him my buying trip is on hold. And I need you to write checks for the bills that are piled on the desk here somewhere. They're right in the ledger . . ."

"You get a few more bites down before you go flyin' outta here, honey."

The phone rang again, and Elsie quickly reached for it.

"I'll get this. You eat. Hello, yes, I do remember speaking to you before, but I'm sorry, Miss Mona has just received distressing family news and can't be takin' calls right now."

Elsie was silent a moment as she listened to the voice on the other end of the line.

"Yes, I do see. I'm sure Miss Mona would be very happy to speak with you."

She lowered the phone and covered the receiver with her hand.

"You need to take this call, honey. It's about Hallie."

Mona offered a silent prayer and reached for the phone.

Chapter Four

Thirty miles down the road, Mona remembered Oscar.

After the call, she'd hollered a few garbled instructions to Elsie as she'd raced up the open staircase separating the front of the shop from the office. She'd pulled her father's army duffel from beneath the walnut four-poster bed and stuffed it with whatever garments were close at hand, slamming drawers and sending unneeded items skittering across the hardwood floor. Oscar had scurried under the bed for refuge, disappearing beneath a corner of the red floral dust ruffle. Minutes later, Mona had slammed the door behind her and pounded down the stairs, leaving a bewildered ten-pound miniature dachshund cowering beneath the bed.

The move to Stewartville had been rough for Oscar. He'd been an unenthusiastic addition to Mona's inheritance when her father passed away the year before Stacy died. The dog had grieved for a year for his master, lying listlessly on the living-room couch and staring out the window. Only Hallie and Stacy had been able to coax back glimmers of Oscar's personality during their summer break. Then Stacy had died, Hallie had left, and Mona had moved to Stewartville. Their first three months, Oscar had spent most of his time under Mona's bed in the loft apartment. At night, he would take up residence at the foot of her four-poster, but every morning, she'd find the dog snuggled into the small of her back under the covers. The only thing Oscar had gotten excited about in Stewartville was his time with Tessa, Elsie's enormous shepherd.

Mona hated to ask Elsie to do one more thing, but there was no choice. Keeping one eye steady on the road, she reached across the seat and rummaged in her purse for her cell.

The phone rang five times before Elsie finally picked up. She was breathing heavily.

"Stewartville Antiques, Elsie McFeeney speaking."

"Elsie, it's Mona. Did I get you from somewhere? You sound like you've been running."

"Well, yes, I was in the back room with Harold, helping him drag in an old chifferobe he'd had in his basement that he wants to refinish for Bessie Newland. But I'll be jiggered if that monster isn't just a bit bigger'n we can manage by ourselves. We were trying to slide it off his truck, nice and slick, and it kinda came a little faster than we thought it would. Sorta pinned his foot. I imagine he'd like me to get back to him quick."

Mona could hear muffled hollering in the background.

"Oh, for heaven's sake, Elsie, I'll call back in ten minutes."

"No, no, long as I'm here, you might as well tell me why you called, but I don't s'pose this would be a good time for swappin' recipes."

Elsie knew Mona didn't have any recipes, unless you counted beef stew from a can.

"I'll make it fast. I can't believe I did this, but I totally forgot Oscar. I wondered if you could take him home tonight when you leave and keep him until I get back. You know how much he loves to be with Tessa, and I don't want him feeling abandoned. I know it's asking a lot, Elsie, but I'm sure he'll be good."

There was more hollering in the background, and Elsie paused for a moment to direct her shrill voice away from the phone and toward the back room.

"Well, that's good, Harold. I was sure we'd get it sooner or later. Now this is Mona with an emergency. You just slip off that boot, and I'll take a look at that toe in a splickety-second."

Mona knew Elsie's splickety-seconds could turn into hours. Elsie's voice dropped a few decibels as she put the phone back near her mouth.

"I'm way ahead of you. I already brought Oscar downstairs to keep me 'n' Harold company in the shop, and Harold took him out to go potty and got him a little treat. You scared him quite a touch by flyin' out the door like that and leavin' your room such a mess. I did pick up a few of your clothes and hung them up. Kinda rearranged 'em a little better for you in the closet. And I told Oscar he's going home with me tonight to spend the night with Tessa, and he's sittin' near the back door in Harold's workroom recliner just waitin' to go."

Mona smiled. She was hugely relieved that Elsie was willing to take him home. A few days with Tessa and with Elsie's grandchildren would be Oscar's own version of summer camp.

"Thanks, Elsie. It means a lot to me. I mean it. When I get back, I owe you a dinner."

Harold hollered again.

"Well, then. Dinner sounds like a good idea, long as it's at Trina's. Harold, I'm comin', don't go gettin' a dander up. And there's one more thing now, and I'm just tellin' you like it is. Phil called back. He transferred five hundred dollars into your ATM account to help cover expenses for whatever comes up in the next week or so with you and that child. I know what you're thinkin', and I made the decision to give him your account number. It was the right thing for him to do as a father, and you need to honor that, not sit there sputterin' about your pride and not takin' help from people. Lord knows you need it right now, and the only thing you need to think about is that girl.

"And the bills here are covered," she continued without so much as a breath. "I went through the books today while things were slow, and we're tight, but we've managed to pay a bit to everyone we owe. We can ride things out for another month or so before we have to figure anything out for sure. All we need is a few more sales every month, and we'll get over this hump."

Mona bit her lip, and for a moment the words wouldn't come. She'd left the shop with her credit card and sixty-three bucks, not even thinking where the rest would come from. She'd always kept a little extra cash stashed at the beach house, basted into the lining of her bedroom curtains, but she couldn't remember if she'd cleaned it out when she'd moved.

"Elsie . . ."

"I'll be hangin' up now so's you can take a little time to thank the Lord for providing for you again, child."

Mona gripped the cell phone tightly as a wave of emotion washed over her. She tried to blink away the tears that had so quickly sprung to life. She *hated* feeling dependent, *hated* feeling like she was taking a handout from Phil and Ellen. But Elsie was right. It was kind for Phil to offer, and it was right for him to offer. So why did it spark a flicker of resentment in her heart?

Her face flushed hot. *You can't accept the thought that you might need anyone except God for anything.*

"Oh, please, Lord, I know we've had this conversation before, but I'd rather not have it again right now. I seem to be painfully aware that at this moment I'm dependent on everybody for every-thing. I'm dependent on Elsie and Harold for taking care of the shop. I'm dependent on Phil and Ellen for putting the next tank of fuel in this bucket of bolts, and I'm dependent on Dan Evans to keep Hallie safe. This, of course, doesn't at all discount the fact that I'm totally dependent on You for the whole ball of wax. It's just that at this moment, I feel like the wax is melting, and I'm coming a bit unglued."

A moment of panic flickered over her as she checked the charge on her phone. *Four bars. Good.* She popped open the glove box and took a quick glance as she searched for her phone cord. It was there. *Amazing.* Her cell phone was her only connection to Hallie at the moment, until she could see for herself that she was safe. She knew that Dan Evans was keeping an eye on her and that he was accessible at the touch of a button, but she had to stifle the urge to call him back. She had to trust him.

The serenity of the countryside slipped unno-ticed past her window as the scarred and dented box truck plowed through the afternoon heat. She knew she couldn't have trusted her aging F-150, which had yet to be unloaded from the Bailey auc-tion, so her only choice had been the truck she used to haul bigger loads. Even with the acceler-ator mashed to the floor, it was giving her only sixty miles an hour downhill. She whispered a silent prayer of thanks that last night Harold had unloaded the estate-sale furniture he was refinishing.

Mona's hair danced around her face, and she distractedly batted it away. The narrow driveway to the beach house would be impassable, and she'd have to leave the truck parked at the foot of the lane. With that thought, her leg tightened and her foot pressed harder to the floor.

"There are no coincidences, Lord. I know that. You're in this, and You were in it before Hallie decided to run. Thank You for Phil's generosity. Thank You for putting Dan on the beach at the crack of dawn for who-knows-what reason, and for giving him the common sense to call me. And for giving Ellen and Phil the grace to let me go to Hallie first when there's no good reason they should. Give me words for a broken child who can't trust You or anybody else. Maybe help me to use my own pain to see into her hurting heart. Help us all somehow to really see You."

The miles flew by with the pleading of Mona's heart, as she fought the urge to press the accelerator through the floorboard. Dan had promised to call if Hallie tried to run or—

Mona refused to let her mind complete the thought. He had promised to stop back by the house and maybe keep Hallie company until Mona got there. She had found his quiet confidence reassuring. His voice had sounded apologetic as he told her he'd been eating his breakfast on her deck at sunrise for the past three weeks since he'd been home from college. He hoped she didn't mind.

Mind? Mind that for some logic-defying reason he'd chosen to entangle himself in a crisis with a runaway fifteen-year-old?

Not that it surprised her. Dan had always been one of her special kids from the neighborhood and one of her favorite English students. Not that she'd admit to having favorites. He'd played an occasional game of beach volleyball with the girls the summer of Stacy's death. He and his mother had been living in the tidy white Cape Cod down the street for less than a year when it happened. Mona doubted that he and Hallie had spoken since. Ellen would have made sure of that. She'd controlled everything about Hallie's life since the funeral, and Muskegon friends had been cut off and discarded like last week's trash.

Like me, Mona thought. *Like we're a part of Hallie's life that never existed.*

Now it seemed they were a part of life that Hallie had chosen to run back to.

Dan's second apology had caught Mona off guard.

"I hope it was okay that I called you first, Miss V. I wasn't sure how to get a hold of Hallie's parents. I just thought it was important for someone to know right away."

59

It was a moment before Mona answered. "You're very thoughtful, Dan. I'm sure Hallie's parents will be grateful you responded so quickly." Mona paused briefly. His intuition had hit close to home.

"She's probably very upset, Dan. Hallie, I mean. I don't think it's a good idea for her to be alone. She's not thinking straight right now. Maybe if you could pretend to drop by, you know, without being obvious, and check to see how she is. Then you could call me on my cell phone if there are any . . . problems, or if she's . . . hurt."

But no call came. And as the box truck lumbered through the countryside, Mona's grip on the phone slowly eased, and her thoughts drifted. She wondered if the Hallie who had greeted Dan on the front porch that morning even remotely reminded him of the child he had known her thirteenth summer, an exuberant, confident tomboy who feared nothing and no one, especially people she was told were older and wiser. Mona had seen her niece's will of steel sharpened during pick-up games of beach volleyball. If one of the older boys attempted an overhand serve, Hallie was right behind him, ready and willing to break her bones trying to duplicate the move. When the college guys nailed a spike shot in her direction, she dug it out, even if it meant a face full of sand and welts on her arms.

Stacy had been quieter, two years younger than

Hallie, but confident beyond her years. She was indifferent to the competitiveness of the beach volleyball tournaments and chose instead to create elaborate sandcastles at the water's edge. As an eleven-year-old, she'd shared an easy rapport with everyone, in spite of their age. Even with her mother, whose sullen sulks would have stymied the efforts of Dr. Phil himself, in Mona's opinion.

I've got to give her to You, Lord. Both of them, actually—well, I guess all of us, if I'm honest. We're all struggling to really believe that Stacy's death wasn't just a huge accident. We all want to say that if we'd just done one thing differently, it wouldn't have happened. We're all drowning in our own guilt.

I only know that if Jesus didn't come to free us from guilt and shame and sin and mistakes and all the pain of our life, then there's nothing about the Christian life that's worth anything. Give me strength through Your truth and the power of Your Spirit to walk in this. Help me to help Hallie believe that she can see herself the way You see her in all of this; that it's hard work, but You've already done the work for us. And help me to believe that Your love can overcome my sister's bitterness and hate. We're in this together, and I'm asking You to help us believe that You're there with us, whether we see it or feel it or not.

The weight of silence echoed through the truck

for the next thirty miles, but Mona sat quietly and let the weight press against her. She knew the silence was just the sound of her heart trying to listen.

Dan's coffee had gone cold, but he didn't move to refill it. Instead, he sat quietly and wondered what he'd gotten himself into. He'd always admired Miss VanderMolen. She'd often gathered the neighborhood kids for cookouts and beach parties, usually when her nieces visited.

Stacy and Hallie's mother had come for the first day of the girls' vacation that last summer. She'd sat on the beach and read Oprah-recommended books and *People* while Miss V spent time teaching the girls to swim and bodysurf. To Dan, Ellen Bowen had seemed aloof, elegant, and overly preoccupied with losing her jewelry in the beach sand. Stacy looked like her mother, slender and blonde, while Hallie resembled her Aunt Mona. Both had the same unruly red hair, Hallie's a long cascade and Miss V's cut chin-length. Dan remembered Hallie laughingly telling him that if he ever wanted to really tick her mother off, to mention that Hallie looked like she could be Aunt Mona's kid.

Dan rose, poured his coffee into the sink, and jotted his mom a note on the magnetic grocery list on the fridge. *Gone to check on something at Miss V's. Back for lunch. Work at one.* Then he headed out the kitchen door and up the path over the dunes to Miss V's back yard.

Dan's strides came in easy measure as he ascended the winding path through the woods. For the past two summers, he'd worked as a lifeguard for the Bible conference that occupied the property between Miss V's house and the Mona Lake channel that emptied into Lake Michigan. Gilead Conference Center drew thousands of people each summer who came for the speakers, the music, and the lake. He had worked most of the time at the pool, which was built directly into the beach sand along the shoreline. But he'd also been trained for the hazards of lake duty and the constant threat of the Lake Michigan undertow. He'd learned that safety was often an illusion and that hesitation often came with regrets. He hurried his pace as he neared Miss V's cottage, remembering her words.

Hurt. Dan knew the implications. He knew Hallie had been on the edge of despair that morning when she'd fled into the house and slammed the door. That had been hours ago. Enough time to . . . get hurt.

He decided the back door would be best and loped down a narrow path through the sword grass. Climbing the wooden stairs to the deck, he approached the crisp, white door, stood directly in line with the peephole, and rapped firmly.

No response.

He waited for what seemed like minutes, then checked his watch. He lifted his hand to knock again just as the door was flung open.

Hallie and Dan stared at each other. He cleared his throat. "Hey, Hal. I thought I saw signs of life down here and just wanted to see what was up." He jammed his hands into his jeans pockets and willed his shoulders to relax.

"Liar."

He wasn't surprised. Hallie had never been one to mince words. He felt his face relax.

"And what is that stupid smile for? You think it's funny to sneak up on me and then the first thing out of your mouth is a lie? I saw you snooping around this morning."

Hallie's hands were planted defiantly on her hips. She wore jean shorts and a bright yellow T-shirt tied in a knot at the waist. Her feet were bare. Her red hair was a mass of curls, slightly mashed on one side, as if she'd been sleeping.

"I see that age hasn't tempered your rudeness, Hallie Bowen. Yes, I did see you this morning, but I was hardly snooping. You seem to have forgotten that the neighborhood association owns this beach and it isn't your personal property. And if I'm out enjoying the sunrise, that's none of *your* business. I came down to the beach to say hello to an old friend, but he wasn't here. I don't suppose it would be asking too much for you to offer me a drink of water?"

Dan tipped his head slightly, as if in challenge. If he had been standing in the kitchen, he would have towered over Hallie by almost a foot. She dropped her gaze and looked at her feet for a moment, then raised her head. Her tone was surprisingly contrite.

"I'm sorry, Dan. You woke me from a nap, and I have a skull-splitting headache. I didn't get much sleep last night. Come on in. Just for a minute."

Dan stepped into the open kitchen, then on into the adjoining living room while Hallie took a vintage Bugs Bunny glass from the red-painted kitchen cupboard and filled it at the sink.

"You can't stay long because I've got some things I've got to get to."

She turned and handed him the drink, and Dan stared into her eyes.

"Liar."

Her gaze dropped again to her feet, and she shifted her weight as she ran her hand through her tangled hair.

"Okay, so we're even. But I'm not going to talk to you about anything, do you understand? I came here because I'm sick and tired of people, so if you're going to stay for even five minutes, you have to agree to shut up. Deal?" She drew circles on the floor with her big toe.

Dan had dropped onto a barstool at the counter separating the living room from the kitchen. He nodded.

"You know, it's considered polite to answer questions when you're asked," Hallie said as she turned to search for ice cubes in the freezer.

"You just told me to shut up," Dan countered. "I guess I'm waiting for you to clarify the ground rules. I assume it's all right for me to sit down while I drink my water?"

"Idiot."

"I'll take that as a yes." Dan drained the glass and set it on the counter.

"You know, your aunt Mona would have a fit if she knew I was on her white carpet with my size fourteens that just collected sand all the way from my place."

"You're done with your water. I think you should leave."

Once again, her hands were on her hips.

"Well, I think I shouldn't," Dan replied softly. "I think I should just sit here for a while and spend some time with an old friend. Maybe take off my sandals out of respect for your aunt."

"Please, please leave," Hallie whispered. The fragility he had seen on her face that morning had crept into her eyes. Her right hand gripped the counter as if she were going to fall.

"Dan, please go."

He searched her face for a moment, then rose and stepped around the counter, within arm's reach of her, as he placed his glass in the sink and turned to scan the beach through the living-room window.

"You know, the front porch steps have always been my favorite spot at your aunt's house. I come here a lot to watch the sunsets and sunrises from those steps, and even though I'm by myself, I never feel alone there."

He turned to face Hallie. "I'd like to sit on the steps with you, Hallie. We don't have to talk, not a word. But I'd like to be with you. I'm not going to leave."

For several moments, the sound of muffled sobs marked the silence. Hallie stared at the floor, tracing more circles with her toe. Finally, she lifted her face to look into the eyes of her friend.

"Yes, I think we can do that."

Chapter Five

Mona parked the box truck on the street near the bottom of the lane and ran toward the beach house. Only seconds passed before she caught a glimpse of the familiar yellow clapboard through the trees as she raced toward the sound of the surf.

Not too shabby for forty-six, she told herself as she paused at the top of the incline, rested her hands on her hips, and gazed at the house. She shoved away the sudden awareness that she hadn't called the place home for a long time. It had been easier to give it over, at least in part, to people who didn't know its secret. So she'd rented it out to the occasional friend-of-a-friend after moving to Stewartville, running back and forth only occasionally to oversee maintenance and cleaning projects.

She wasn't sure when she had stopped thinking of it as home. Home was about family, and no one from her family had crossed the Muskegon County line since Stacy died. The house had sat empty for months at a time. Tonight would be the first time she would sleep in the beach house since she'd moved to Stewartville.

The tiny house had been Mona's pride and joy, bought with a portion of her inheritance money shortly after her father died. She'd gutted the interior herself and torn off the dilapidated porch that had succumbed to the unrelenting cycle of sun, sand, and snow. She'd contracted the interior work and insisted on keeping the spaces light, airy, and colorful to highlight her collection of antique treasures. She'd chosen only the very dearest of those possessions to take to Stewartville. Others had been put in storage or packed away for the day that Hallie might take an interest in family mementos. Ellen certainly never would.

Mona found the back door unlocked and slipped inside. Except for a glass sitting in the sink and a huge pair of sandals near the door to the front deck, the house appeared to be unoccupied. The pillows on the red buffalo-plaid sofa were scrunched on one end, as if someone had rested there, but there was no sign of Hallie or Dan. She listened momentarily for the sounds of movement in the loft, then quickly checked the two downstairs bedrooms.

The master bedroom was empty, but a black leather jacket and motorcycle helmet were tossed across the antique quilt on the oak bed in the guest room. Turning from the bedroom, Mona wondered how her niece would react when she realized Dan had ratted her out. She'd seen enough of Hallie's rages to know their fury, but she'd never been the object of one.

As she stepped into the living room, she caught her first glimpse of Hallie and Dan through the bay window. They were sitting on the porch steps, still as statues, staring at the horizon, their shoulders almost touching, but not quite. The only sound was the soft cadence of the waves whispering through the open front door. Mona walked quietly toward the window and watched in silence for several minutes, uncertain what to do next.

"I know you're there, Aunt Mona. I heard the back door open and close."

Hallie stood, brushed the sand from her shorts, then walked slowly across the porch and slid open the screen door.

Mona's eyes swept her niece's face and studied her red and swollen eyes. There were no tears, and for a moment Mona's heart froze. Then, with a steady sureness, she stepped toward Hallie and the two fell into a long embrace as Dan watched awkwardly from the steps. Hallie's head rested against her aunt's shoulder as Mona gently stroked her niece's long red hair and the two rocked imperceptibly. Hallie made no move to pull away, and Mona whispered a silent prayer of thanks.

Over Hallie's shoulder, Mona watched as Dan stood and jammed his hands into the pockets of his jeans, clearing his throat to break the silence.

"Good to see you, Miss V. Hallie and I were just enjoying the view for a minute before I had to get to work. I'm sorry to rush away, but I'm scheduled to guard at one, and I promised my mom I'd get home in time to have a bite of lunch with her."

Hallie broke free from Mona's embrace and whirled to face Dan, her eyes blazing. Mona could see she was furious.

"You called her, didn't you? How dare you come in here with your stupid story about sitting on the steps, when all you were doing was spying, you rotten liar!"

"Hallie!" Mona broke in before Dan had a chance to reply. "Stop it! Of course he called me. What would you expect him to do? You cruise in here by yourself in the middle of the night on your father's motorcycle, no license, no permission, no respect for people who love you, break into my house, and you're mad at Dan? What gives you the right to get angry at people trying to protect you? You could have been killed. In fact I'm toying with the idea of throttling you right now, so don't you dare take it out on him."

Mona's tone was low and even, but her green eyes were narrow, and they were locked on Hallie's face. She leaned forward as she spoke, her hands on her hips in a pose that mirrored her niece's stance. It was a look and a tone she'd used to back down high school linemen twice her size, and even an overambitious date once or twice. But it was a tone Hallie had never before felt directed at her. The words seemed to stun her, and she stood speechless, tears streaming down her face.

In her peripheral vision, Mona saw Dan head toward the living-room door, reach in and grab his sandals, then sit back down on the deck stairs to pull them on. She never so much as glanced in his direction, but she was surprised when he spoke.

"I'm not sorry at all, Hallie. I did what I thought a friend should do for a friend. If you don't appreciate that, that's your problem. I was hoping you'd be old enough to understand. And for the record, I didn't lie. I did want to be with you."

He nodded to Mona and moved down the front steps. "I have to go, Miss V. Stop by and see my mom if you get the chance. I know she'd want to see you." Then he disappeared around the side of the house.

Mona wrapped her arms around Hallie's rigid shoulders and drew her into the living room, closing the door behind them. She kicked off her sandals and pulled Hallie gently toward the kitchen.

"I barely ate any lunch, and I'm starved. I've got some things in the truck that should be brought up and put away, but I'm sure not going to cook for us tonight, surprise, surprise. I thought we'd head down to Smitty's and get some fish and onion rings and eat them on the channel wall down by the Coast Guard station. We could watch the boats heading in from the Big Lake, maybe talk a little."

Hallie was silent, brushing away the tears that continued to flow.

"I don't want to fight, Hal. I just need to know you're really okay. I'm not the enemy, and neither is Dan. I think you know that." She stroked Hallie's hair as she spoke.

Mona could see Hallie's hands twisting the knot in her T-shirt as she stared at the floor.

"You aren't shipping me home to Mom and Dad? They're not going to be waiting for me at Smitty's or here when we get back?"

"Is that what you want? Do you want your parents to come?"

"No!" The word exploded from Hallie's lips.

Mona paused for a moment. "You know, you scared your parents half to death, Hal. What you did was totally selfish and hurt them in a way I can only begin to understand. But I think you came here for a reason, and I know you can't be left alone. If you want to stay for a while, it will have to be on my terms, and only if I get the okay for those terms from your parents."

Mona waited in silence and let the words soak in.

"I left my truck at the bottom of the lane. I want you to bring the groceries up while I make a few calls. I also brought a duffel and a canvas tote with some business papers in it that I'd like you to get while I go into the bedroom. I promised your folks I'd call right away."

Hallie twisted the knot more tightly.

"They let me come after you, Hal. By myself. I'm not sure I could have been that gracious if I were in their shoes."

"Gracious, right," Hallie muttered. "Look up the word in the dictionary, and I'm sure you'll find my mother's picture."

"And does the sarcasm help?" Mona asked softly.

Hallie slipped free of her aunt's arms, shoved her feet into the sandals she'd slid under the couch, and headed out the back door. Mona stood frozen, listening for the sound of a motorcycle engine roaring to life. When it didn't come, she went into her bedroom and closed the door. As she punched the familiar number into her cell phone, a familiar throb began a pulsating rhythm behind her eyes. She pressed her fingers into her temples and closed her eyes as she leaned back against the closed door.

Mona wondered whether Hallie could hear the one-sided phone conversation as she brought in the packages, then the huge canvas duffel and the tote. She could hear the sounds of her niece putting away the bagels, fresh strawberries, watermelon, crunchy wheat bread, chips, lunchmeat, chocolate doughnuts, and a huge bag of peanut M&M's. No one had ever accused Mona of being a health-food freak. She had once told Hallie and Stacy that it was her sacred trust as an aunt to pass on her passion for chocolate in all forms to her nieces. Mona's sugar indulgences with the girls would have made Ellen pass out if she'd known.

Mona spoke to her sister for several minutes, her voice crescendoing, then dropping as she willed herself to remain calm and rational. The throb in her head escalated to a reverberating thud as the moments passed. The stakes were too high this time, she'd told herself before she'd phoned. So when Ellen inexplicably relented, Mona suddenly found herself speechless. With one deep breath, she opened the door and walked into the kitchen.

"Your dad would like to speak to you for a moment, Hallie."

Mona watched her niece grimace as she slid a canister of lemonade mix into the pantry cupboard. That her dad wanted to talk would mean one of two things to Hallie. Either her mother had freaked out so badly that she couldn't be rational, or her dad was so angry he was insisting on speaking to Hallie himself. Neither scenario would make her want to rush to the phone, but Mona gave her no choice. She pushed her gently down onto a barstool and placed the phone in her hand. Hallie drew her feet up to the highest rung and encircled her knees with her arms.

"Hey, Dad."

"Hallie, are you all right?"

He was working to keep his tone even, but Mona could hear his words from where she sat next to Hallie, her arm draped around her shoulder. Considering his daughter had run away in the middle of the night on his sixteen-thousand-dollar motorcycle, Mona thought he was doing pretty well.

"Yeah, Dad, I'm sorry. I didn't do this to hurt you and Mom. I just had to get away. Your bike's all right. I put it in Aunt Mona's shed and covered it with a sheet."

"I don't care about the stupid bike, Hallie. Your mom and I just need to know you're safe. We need you back, honey . . . not just here at home. We need *you* back . . ."

Hallie hated crying. Mona knew it, anybody who knew Hallie knew it, but almost instantly the tears were dripping from her chin.

"I don't think the old Hallie is in there anymore, Dad." Her voice was barely a whisper. "If she is, I don't know where to find her. I thought maybe I could find her here, where I lost her."

For a long time, Mona heard only the sounds of her own breathing and Hallie's quiet sobs.

"We love you, Hallie. Your mom and I want you to know that more than anything. We'll do anything to help you, if you'll just tell us what it is." Mona heard Phil's voice break, followed by a deep breath. "Now let me talk to your aunt Mona again."

Hallie handed over the phone and sat quietly at the breakfast bar, her head in her hands.

"So we'll go with that plan then, Phil, unless something comes up." Mona gave Hallie's shoulder a gentle shove and whispered, "We're going out to dinner. I just need to lie down for ten minutes first." Then back into the phone, "Right, right, Phil. Of course I will. We'll call tomorrow. You've got my cell number." With a click, it was over, and she shoved the cell phone into her pocket.

"Looks like we're going to dinner, kiddo. Just give me ten minutes to lie down and get rid of the cannon factory that's exploding inside my brain, and I'll show you how an old lady on a Harley can make the neighbors stare."

Mona stood thigh deep in the lake, her pink ter-rycloth robe heavy with the weight of the swirling water tugging at her legs. At first the robe had floated on the surface as she'd waded in to her ankles, then to her knees. But as she'd inched her way deeper, it had slipped beneath the surface and gripped her legs, growing heavier with each step.

From the shore, a voice called out, but Mona did not turn. She knew the voice, the tone, but she continued to inch her way into the water, the palms of her hands caressing the gentle crests now tugging at her pink sleeves.

Once again, the voice called and again Mona gave no response. Her eyes never flickered from the object of her gaze: a woman in a matching pink robe sitting neatly cross-legged in an over-sized flowerpot, busily crocheting a deep red afghan as the waves lifted, then lowered her with their swells.

The waves shimmered in flashes of gold and pink where Mona's fingers skimmed the water. A pulsating light emanated from behind her with increasing brightness, but the woman in the flow-erpot remained intent on her needlework as Mona inched her way forward.

The light burned into Mona's back, and the gold and pink shimmers glared in painful shards that pierced her eyes. The voice on the beach grew louder, the tone commanding. The woman in the flowerpot raised her head and held Mona in her gaze, her eyes sweeping her face. A hint of a smile played at the corners of her mouth. Then she winked and was gone.

The deafening shriek of sirens slammed into Mona's ears, and she faced the shoreline. Three ambulances edged the water, lined up like limos at an awards ceremony, their doors opened. Her father stood near the open door of the first ambulance, calling and beckoning to Mona, but his voice was drowned out by the roar of the sirens.

Her sleeves were drenched, and her hands had slipped beneath the surface of the water. Her body was stone cold and heavy, and the pink robe had encased her legs. Something was gripping her ankles, and she felt her footing slowly giving way.

In the very instant when the cold overtook her and her feet gave way, she again found herself facing the expanse of the water, the shore behind her, the screaming sirens gone silent. She searched the waves for the woman in the flowerpot, but she was no longer there. Instead, facing each other astride a yellow air mattress, Hallie and Stacy bobbed on the surface of the waves, laughing and winking at each other.

The pulsating light throbbed once again as Stacy slipped from the mattress and beneath the surface of the water.

Then it was over.

When Mona woke up, the headache was gone, but a familiar sense of unease lingered. A glance at her watch told her she had slept for an hour, but she felt oddly fatigued.

In spite of Hallie's protests, she insisted they change into long jeans before hauling the Fat Boy out of the shed. She found an extra helmet, one she'd kept from a brief stint as a biker several years before when Phil had loaned her one of his smaller, older motorcycles. For two exhilarating summers, she'd enjoyed spitting up gravel on back roads and cruising the lakeshore highways. When she'd moved to Stewartville and the loft apartment without a garage, she'd given the motorcycle back. But the love of riding had never left her blood.

"Hang on, girl," Mona shouted, revving the engine and roaring down the tree-canopied lane with a burst of speed that nearly flipped Hallie off the seat.

Hallie grabbed Mona's waist as they burst onto the circle drive, waving one hand at a cluster of wide-eyed neighbors congregated on a white-railed front porch.

They headed north along residential streets shrouded by maples and oaks that cast flickering shadows across the pavement. Mona wondered if Hallie knew where they were heading. Mona's weakness had always been Smitty's, a greasy spoon at Pere Marquette Park, known for its breaded onion rings and Lake Michigan perch. Along with chocolate, perch and onion rings rounded out Mona's addictions, unless you counted the late summer black sweet cherries she indulged in when they were in season.

In one final, graceful curve between two high

dunes, the road fell away to the west, and the lake reappeared, a glimmering ribbon stretching to the horizon. Mona scanned the beach to the north for the familiar red lighthouse marking the Pere Marquette breakwater, a silent sentinel punctuating the sky at the outstretched south arm of Muskegon harbor. They sped past shoreline pavilions, and Mona inhaled deeply the aroma of grilling hamburgers intermingled with pungent wafts of freshwater surf.

They placed their order for carryout at a drive-up window at a ramshackle building barely big enough to rival a full-size car. Smitty's nestled in a wedge of tarmac where the shoreline road arced into a curve that traced the channel wall and the beach for half a mile, then turned back toward the restaurant in one giant oval. For years, the area had been known as the Ovals to locals, although its official name was Pere Marquette Park, named after the pioneering French clergyman who had helped settle the area. The food came quickly, and Mona gave Hallie the task of balancing the steaming bags on her thighs as they cruised a short distance to a rustic pavilion adjacent to the channel wall.

Muskegon Lake was joined to Lake Michigan by a two-hundred-yard-wide, man-made river encased in thick concrete walls. Stretching for almost a mile, the channel provided boating access from Muskegon Lake out into Lake

Michigan. The USS *Silversides*, a retired submarine and popular tourist attraction, rested in dry dock along the south channel wall. On summer afternoons, the concrete walkway was peppered with people who came to watch the parade of boats passing between the two lakes. Just two hundred yards across the channel lay North Muskegon State Park, but by land it was twenty miles distant on roads that skirted the edge of Muskegon Lake before doubling back to Lake Michigan.

The channel harbor was protected by two expansive stretches of concrete on the north and south shores, extending into the waters of Lake Michigan like the embracing arms of a mother. On the south side, the breakwater of Pere Marquette Park provided a wide concrete walkway leading almost a third of a mile out into the lake and to the lighthouse that dominated the harbor. On the north side of the channel, a more primitive breakwater protruded above the waterline in a jagged profile of heaped-up concrete slabs leading to a second, smaller lighthouse. Together, the two lighthouses marked the mouth to the harbor of Muskegon Lake.

The Fat Boy glided gently to a standstill as Mona maneuvered it into a parking space beneath a street light. She had chosen this spot of shoreline because she knew it was one of the few places along the beach that held no memories of Stacy. It was simply a pavilion, not a place where the family had picnicked or swum or argued or played beach volleyball. It was safe.

Mona and Hallie sat together on top of a picnic table facing the channel, the greasy boxes of fish and onions between them. From the pockets of her leather jacket, Mona pulled the two Diet Cokes she'd grabbed from the grocery sack before they'd left the house, sliding one into her niece's hand in silence. Then she fixed her eyes on an unseen object across the channel. For a long time, the sounds of the lake enfolded them, and they took refuge in the conversations of passersby and the preoccupation of food. Hallie was the first to speak, her voice hollow and flat.

"You probably hate me."

Her words once again triggered the tone in Mona's voice that Hallie had so seldom heard.

"Hallie, don't say stupid things. I'm too tired, and you're too smart. I've never allowed you lie to me, and I'm not about to start now. I could never hate you."

Mona took a long swallow of her Diet Coke, set it down at the edge of the table, and drew Hallie into her arms. The child's rigid shoulders and fixed gaze spoke louder than any words.

"I can't go home," she whispered.

"Nobody's sending you home, baby."

"Promise? Tell me you promise." The intensity of her words sent a chill through Mona.

"Hallie, I promise that tonight you and I are going to camp out in the living room and eat until we explode. Then we're going to watch chick flicks and do our nails and maybe even order in pizza and take bets on how long it takes the pizza boy to find our house. And in the morning, I'm packing you off in the truck with me for a buying trip, if you think you can stand the excitement. After that, we'll just make it up as we go along.

"But Hal, at the end of this, you're going to have to face what drove you here. You ran away because you're tired of running away."

Mona lifted Hallie's chin until their eyes met. Again, there was no answer. Then again, the whisper.

"You know I killed her."

It was the first time Hallie had ever breathed the words, words that seared themselves into Mona's heart because for too long they had been her own words.

In that moment, their pain became one. They sat enveloped in the late-afternoon heat, sharing their wounds, tracing one another's scars, not marking the passing hours. When the pain had ebbed with their shared tears, Mona guided her niece back to the motorcycle and waited for her to slip onto the seat behind her. Mona wasn't sure when, but somewhere in the unmarked afternoon hours, the rigidness had ebbed from Hallie's body. The wind would whip away the tears as they drove home through the early twilight toward the beach house. Hallie's arms gripped Mona tightly as they made their way into the darkness.

Chapter Six

Like a hunter stalking its prey, the dream returned.

First the screams, then the choking plea that reverberated over and over again in a crescendo of terror.

Then the hand, rising above the roiling waters, clenching and unclenching as it flailed against the turbid waves. Interlaced among the fingers was the necklace, the gemstones sparkling against the gold, heart-shaped filigree.

D for diamond. E for emerald. A for amethyst. R for ruby. E for emerald. S for sapphire. T for topaz.

Dearest. My dearest Stacy.

Finally, the hand pummeling the surface and slipping forever beneath the murky water as everything faded to black.

Mona wasn't sure what time they'd finally fallen to sleep, but she was the first to wake, long before dawn washed the first streaks of mauve across the sky. She had kept the door to her room ajar so she would hear Hallie's first stirrings, and she lay on her side so she could watch her niece through the crack in the door.

The alarm clock on her nightstand was glowing 6:07 when she heard Hallie awake in her nest of blankets on the living-room floor. The night air had been damp, and Mona watched as Hallie heaved back the red cotton throw, wadded it, and lobbed it into a basket stashed beneath an antique, treadle sewing machine. She stood and stretched her lanky five-foot-eight-inch frame before slipping into white shorts beneath her oversized Winnie-the-Pooh T. Then she turned toward the sliding doors to the front deck and eased them aside as she slid her slender frame through the narrow opening. She paused for a moment, then straddled the railing at the edge of the deck, sitting with one leg planted on the porch, the other dangling above the space that fell away with the slope of the dune. A gentle breeze stirred her hair as she swung her leg slowly to an unheard rhythm.

Mona tossed back the yellow summer coverlet and slipped from her bed. She grabbed a pink robe from a brass hook behind the door and threw it over her shoulders, her eyes still glued to Hallie. Words from last night still rang in her ears, the final words she'd spoken before they'd gotten on the Harley and headed back to the house.

"If that's the lie you're going to choose to believe, Hallie, then let's be totally honest. We all killed Stacy. Your mother killed her because she trusted me to take care of both of you and I didn't. Your father killed her because he was away from his family on business, just like every other summer. And I killed her because I couldn't get to her fast enough . . . because I . . . chose to come back to the house and leave you two alone."

Her voice had trembled and broken, dissolving into gentle gasps as she'd gripped Hallie's hands in both of her own, but her steady gaze had never left the child's face. It was a truth she'd lived with every day of her life since the day Stacy had died. She'd been responsible for the girls. She'd chosen to walk back to the house to get the sunscreen, to leave them for less than five minutes. If she'd been there, she would have seen Stacy go under. She was the adult who was responsible, not this tormented child.

Lord, I know we could all be swallowed alive by the "what ifs." It's only by Your grace that I haven't. I don't know why You allowed Stacy to drown, why all the details of that day had to fall together in that precise order. I don't know why I had to forget the sunscreen or why there had to be a riptide that day. I don't know why Hallie had to watch her sister drown, but I believe You chose to allow us to endure this because You knew it could change us in some way You could use.

And in the moments when the "what ifs" wash over me and drag me under, help me to believe it again.

Mona walked through the kitchen and into the living room, stopping near the sliding doors to the deck. Beyond Hallie, a soft breeze rippled through the knee-high sword grass that covered the dunes in random clusters. Their first summer with Mona, the girls had learned how marram grass came to earn its local name, as they ran over the undulating hills, the softly serrated edges of the slender stalks slicing their legs. Beauty that stung. It had been a startling revelation to the children.

But Mona had taken every opportunity to point out the wonders of the beauty that embraced her duneside home. She looked for ways to teach the girls that creation was a gift from a loving God, whose breath blew across His creation, bringing the cycle of seasons. That God was in control of the world and had designed a special plan for their lives, and that He was the giver of all good things.

She knew that Hallie had believed it for a time.

Then Stacy's death had stripped Hallie of those things. Stripped her of hope; stripped her of faith. The lies had taken root deeply. If there was a God, He was a taker. He enjoyed inflicting pain and destroying people's lives. And no matter how much Aunt Mona had loved her and loved Stacy, she was a fool for clinging to a God who was a monster.

Hallie's face turned ever so slightly, and for a moment Mona thought she had heard her. But her attention was directed elsewhere, over the rise of a small dune north toward the Gilead beach. A man with a slow, rolling gait was crisscrossing the sand with geometric precision. He wore a carpenter's nail belt tied around faded blue dungarees and a shirt of nondescript color. The nail belt accentuated a broad waist, far broader than would have been thought possible for his short frame. He moved with the deliberation of an old man whose knees had carried too much weight for too much time, and he waved an angular metal rod in broad swaths in front of him as he walked. As he moved closer, Mona could see the frayed, green Michigan State University hat that shaded his eyes.

Lum.

Mona couldn't believe he was still alive and still combing his circuit along the beaches. For as long as she could remember, Lum had swept the area beaches with his metal detector, walking a circuit from park to park throughout the summer, staring only at the ground in front of him, speaking to no one. No one knew where he lived or what he did when the bone-chilling winter months set in, but during the summer, people set their watches by him. It was Thursday, his day for the stretch of shoreline from Gilead Bible Conference grounds south to Hoffmaster State Park and back. In three hours he would pass down their stretch of beach again, this time heading north back toward the narrow channel near Gilead that connected Lake Michigan to Mona Lake.

Lum froze and stared in the direction of the house. For a moment, the swinging rhythm of Hallie's legs ceased. Then she turned as another movement caught her attention.

Dan Evans loped down a narrow dune path toward the beach, a paper bag in his hand.

Suddenly Hallie swung her leg back over the rail, squatted, and sat cross-legged on the deck where she could watch the two men, obscured from their view.

If Hallie had been expecting a scene from a prime-time TV drama to unfold, it had to be rather anticlimactic, Mona decided. Dan handed Lum the bag, murmured a few words that Mona couldn't hear, and then headed back up the dune, disappearing into the woods. Lum continued down the beach toward the state park, finally opening the bag just before he disappeared from view around a gentle bend in the shore.

It was several moments before Hallie stood. And for reasons she didn't quite understand, Mona slipped back into the bedroom and pretended she hadn't seen a thing.

Mona's hair whipped her face as the wind danced through the cab of the box truck. Hallie had tamed her mass of curls by twisting them into a knot at the nape of her neck and securing the thick rope with a wide gold clip at the top of her head. Both women were dressed in jean shorts, sandals, and fresh T-shirts that read "Stewartville Antiques, Treasures from the Past to Cherish for Tomorrow." The back of Mona's legs were already sticking to the blue vinyl upholstery, and she envisioned the layer of skin she would leave behind when they arrived in Applington and she peeled herself off the seat. The temperature had risen to a muggy eighty-five, and radio reports promised highs in the mid-nineties.

Conversation was slow for the first fifty miles as they headed north up U.S. Route 31, with the lush green of pines and summer foliage sweeping past their open windows. The tinny radio blared tunes from the sixties as they munched a breakfast of granola bars, watermelon chunks, string cheese, and Diet Coke. Hallie leaned back in her seat, her bare feet propped against the dusty dashboard in an effort to minimize contact between her skin and the sweaty plastic. She slapped at a half-dozen or so flies that seemed annoyingly attracted to Mona's purse, which lay on the seat between them. Hallie hadn't spoken a word since they'd pulled onto the highway, but silence didn't bother Mona. She knew her niece's words would come when she was ready. At least words worth listening to.

Mona's elbow rested on the window ledge. Unconsciously, she fingered a wide silver band that hung from her neck on a matching silver chain, slipping her ring finger into the band, then spinning it with her thumb. She suddenly felt Hallie's eyes on her.

"You're staring at me. Do I look that terrible? I know I'm sweating like a pig." Mona glanced in the rearview mirror. "Jeez Louise, I could make a plastic surgeon run screaming!"

Her eyes were bloodshot and puffy, and the soft furrows that fanned out from the corners of her eyes had deepened, seemingly overnight. The ring dropped from her finger, resting again against her T-shirt as she pressed her hand to her forehead and tried to sweep away the wrinkles.

"Dig around in my purse a bit, Hal, and see if you can find my mascara and compact. I've aged ten years in the past twenty-four hours. Girl, you owe me a spa day and about ten pounds of Godiva."

Hallie dumped the rather impressive contents of Mona's huge purse into her lap.

"Oh man, you've got a moldy hamburger wrapped up in your purse, Aunt Mona! That's just disgusting."

Mona brightened. "I thought I gave that to Oscar last week. Well, that explains the clouds of bugs swarming me lately." She laughed as she slapped a fly on the seat near Hallie's leg, then flicked it onto the floor.

Hallie made a gagging noise. "You've got to be kidding. I'm never gonna eat a hamburger again." She shoved the burger and wrapper into a plastic bag advertising the Curl Up and Dye Hair Salon that was hanging from a radio knob, then extricated the mascara and compact from the pile in her lap and began to shovel the contents back into the purse. Once again, the conversation lagged.

Mona turned off the radio, and the truck went silent except for the wind beating through the windows. *If silence is what Hallie wants, she'll get it,* Mona told herself. She remembered that she'd needed silence, too, to give shape to her words after Stacy had died, to help her hear something beyond herself. The still, small voice of truth had nearly been drowned out by the raging of her heart. Now only the rumble of the engine separated her from her niece. Just as they crossed the county line heading north, Hallie broke the silence. Mona had expected her to start at the edges and work her way in, but the words startled her.

"After Gram died, did you hate Grandpa for getting rid of her stuff so soon? Mom told me he just boxed everything up one day and had somebody haul it all away. Even her wedding china. Mom always loved Gram's wedding china."

Hallie slammed her palm on a fly that had landed on her knee. "The day that somebody touches Stacy's stuff, I'll kill them." She flicked the bug toward the window, and the wind caught it and sucked it away.

Mona glanced at her niece's face. Hallie stared

at the floor as she folded her arms across her chest. Her hands gripped her elbows, her arms drawn in tight to her body as if her stomach ached.

Mona chose her words slowly. "And where did that question come from?"

"You're not the only one with permission to play shrink. I want to know about the ring. You never take it off." Hallie's gaze bored into the floor as she drew her arms even closer.

Mona moved her hand to the silver band and rubbed the cool metal between her thumb and forefinger. "I've had it for a long time, Hal. I'm sure you must have noticed it before this."

"Yeah, I guess so. But it's not like I paid much attention when I was a kid. I've barely seen you in two years."

"Well, it's no big secret. I haven't had it off since the day Grandpa gave it to me at Gram's funeral. He gave your mom Grandma's engagement ring the same day he gave the band to me. I'm sure she's shown it to you."

Hallie snickered. "Right. During one of our mother-daughter bonding moments. Maybe it was one of the nights I was holding her head while she was puking, so she wouldn't pass out in the toilet."

"Hallie!"

"Oh, give me a break. Like I'm telling you something you don't already know or haven't had to do yourself."

Mona glanced again at Hallie. She was staring at her knees, picking imaginary lint from her jeans.

"I found it once when I was going through her stuff. She keeps it in a black velvet bag in a drawer in her armoire with the first engagement ring dad gave her. The one she wore before she got the hernia-maker she wears now."

Hallie paused, and Mona ignored the urge to fill the silence. Hallie shifted her weight and scrunched down in the seat.

"Gram's diamond is too small for an appropriate status symbol, and we both know Mother Dear is hardly into sentimentality. That rock she made Dad buy her is just something to wave in her friends' faces at the country club. And you're ignoring my question."

"Really? I'd hoped you hadn't noticed." Mona tried to force a smile, but it didn't come. Her eyes stared straight ahead as she gripped the wheel with one hand and fingered her mother's ring with the other. Her eyes felt suddenly hot, and she was aware of a gentle throb behind her eyes.

"Yes, it was hard. Mostly because my father never asked me if there was anything of Gram's I wanted. One day it was all just gone, pieces of her that I wanted to touch again, to hold. It felt like he gave away the last parts of her that I could keep close to me. It hurt a lot, really." It was the first time Mona had actually spoken the words out loud. She swallowed and was surprised at the tightness gripping her neck, constricting her throat.

"Did you ever forgive him?"

The pause was long, and Hallie repeated the question.

"I want to know if you've forgiven him. I don't think I could have. Some things people do aren't worth forgiving."

At that moment, Mona saw the power of the lie strangling her niece's heart.

"Maybe I'm still forgiving him." The band dropped to Mona's chest as the wind choreographed the strands of hair that danced around her face. "I wear the necklace to keep Gram close to my heart, but I also wear it to remind me to forgive my dad. I need to be reminded a lot, sometimes every day. And then there's the most important reason."

"The most important reason?"

"To help me remember what's in my own heart. The things I hide there. The things I have to work to forgive myself for."

Hallie went pale and turned abruptly toward the window, swallowed in sudden silence. Mona let her be.

She saw that her words had pierced Hallie's heart, reminding her of what she was working so hard to hide, what Mona knew—that from the first horrible moments after Stacy's death, that Hallie had died, too, devoured piece by piece by a beast as ravenous as the Lake Michigan undertow. As surely as Stacy had been pulled from their grasp that day, Hallie had been ripped away, too, bound by a millstone of guilt, the same guilt that tore at all of them.

Mona prayed for gentleness as she spoke the question she knew Hallie needed to answer.

"And what about you? Who do you have to forgive?"

Hallie kept her face turned toward the window, and for the next hour, all Mona could see was the back of her bowed head and the cascading curls tugging at the restraint of the gold barrette. Mona never asked again, and an answer never came.

But she knew the answer.

Only hours ago, she had held the writhing, screaming girl in her arms as her nightmares had ravaged the night. Over and over, the screams had filled the night air as Hallie's arms had pummeled the invisible waves.

Hallie had to forgive herself. They all had to forgive themselves.

Chapter Seven

Dead bugs. For the first time in her life, Mona was grateful for a windshield slimed with green and yellow splatters. Hallie was scouring them from the glass when the call came, just as Mona was sliding thirty bucks across the gas station's cracked Formica counter. She watched through a streaky window as Hallie dragged a dripping squeegee through a glob of yellow goo, muttering something Mona was glad she couldn't hear. She wished she could say the same for Ellen, whose shrill tones bombarded her the moment she clicked the phone on. She was certain the cashier could hear every word.

"I've changed my mind. Phil and I have decided to come to Muskegon today to pick Hallie up and bring her home."

Mona stifled her first response to hang up and turn the phone off. *Let them come,* she thought. *They don't know where in the blue blazes we are.*

Instead, she drew a deep breath and counted slowly to five before speaking. She'd learned a long time ago that three just wasn't enough when she was talking to Ellen.

"That really won't work, Ellen, for several reasons. First of all, Hallie and I aren't even in Muskegon. We're on a buying trip, and we won't be getting back until quite late tonight." She made a mental note to extend the day's activities, maybe window shopping and a sunset in Ludington. "Besides, Hallie isn't ready yet. She's barely speaking. If you give her a few days and let her feel like she's got a little space, it will be better for everyone."

Mona tried to visualize her sister's response. She pictured her sitting at the imported French writing desk in the corner of the gold-and-Tiffany-blue master suite, drumming freshly manicured nails and shooting death glances at her husband. Phil would be staring out the french doors, conjuring visions of his own escape.

"And I suppose you think spending time with you is what she needs right now, instead of being with us? Because when it comes to what's right and wrong for everybody, you've got a corner on the market, right?" Ellen's tone was cutting.

Mona's throat tightened and something in her chest went fire-hot. She considered hanging up, but she forced herself to keep her voice even.

"And what do you think she needs, Ellen? New shrinks to add to the half dozen you've already taken her to? More drugs? Maybe a shopping trip to the Somerset Collection? For heaven's sake, she's a walking time bomb. This is Hallie's *life* we're talking about! Try to forget for just one minute that you can't stand the thought that she's with me right now."

The gray-haired clerk behind the counter cleared his throat and turned to rearrange a cigarette display on a wire spinner. Mona glanced around the tiny room, then headed for a chipped white door marked "Ladies," closing and locking it behind her.

Ellen was strangely quiet at the other end of the line, and for a moment Mona thought she had hung up.

"El, are you still there?"

"I can't believe you could be so ugly to me right now."

Mona sighed and rolled her eyes. It felt like junior high all over again. But then, it had never really stopped feeling that way between them. Conversations with Ellen had always felt like a tightrope walk over a minefield, with Mona the only one ever falling and getting blown up.

"I'm sorry. I really am, but I need you to listen to me. Last night I promised your daughter she wouldn't have to go home right away. I made that promise because you and Phil agreed to leave her with me for a while. You *told* me to tell her she could stay, and she knows that. If you don't live up to your word on this, you'll lose even more of her than you've already lost. I can't let you do that to yourself or to her. I couldn't care less if you get mad at me. You are *not* coming to get her today, and you're *not* coming to get her tomorrow, do you understand?"

"And how do you think you're going to stop me?" The voice was icy.

Mona leaned wearily against a scarred paneled wall and rested her head in her hands.

"I'm not going to stop you, Ellen. You're going to stop yourself, because you know it's what's best for Hallie right now. You're going to make a choice that's hard for you because you know it's right for your daughter. That's what parents do.

You're going to honor your word to her and wait. No matter how hard it is for you."

Seconds ticked by as Mona waited for her sister's response. Someone knocked at the door, but she ignored it.

"Maybe it's time for you to start believing a few hard things, too. You're not her mother, Mona. That would be a good place to start, no matter how hard it might be for you. You've always found ways to make them love you more. It's one of the reasons I hate you."

Mona felt as if she'd been slapped. She'd come to expect it, but it always took her breath away.

"Yes, Ellen. I know." She exhaled slowly, struggling to control the sob that rose in her chest as she waited for an answer.

"The Fourth of July. Ten days, then we're coming to get her."

It was more than Mona had hoped for. She only hoped it would be enough.

The phone conversation left her shaken, and the knocking on the bathroom door continued for several minutes before Mona emerged and muttered an embarrassed *sorry* to a dismayed-looking ten-year-old clutching her mother's hand and shifting her weight from foot to foot.

Mona reassured herself as she walked to the truck. She had a plan. She wasn't sure if it was a good one or a bad one, since she was simply making it up as she went along. But so far, Hallie hadn't been arrested and hadn't tattooed or pierced anything on Mona's watch, or run off with the circus. That had to count for some measure of success, to Mona's way of thinking . . . even if she wasn't totally sure about the tattoos or piercing.

They headed back down the road again. Hallie commented that Mona might want to consider letting up a bit on the Diet Coke so that small children could have a chance to go potty, too, and then they had fallen back into a comfortable silence.

They meandered through western Michigan, stopping at estate sales Mona had circled in the papers she'd picked up at the gas station. The plan was to stop for lunch and maybe a walk on the Pere Marquette breakwater. And if she prayed real hard and held her mouth just right, maybe, just maybe Hallie might choose to pretend she didn't know the real plan. The plan to coax open her heart, maybe even to persuade her to talk about the death screams that had sent Mona flying from her bed last night.

Ten miles down the road from the gas station, they hit their first bit of luck. At a community yard sale held on the front lawn of a tiny Methodist church, Mona found the perfect oak sideboard for Ginny Mae, at half the price the dealer had paid at the Bailey auction. They'd loaded it and pulled back onto the road before Mona realized she was suddenly grateful for the irritating man who'd bid her up. She knew the piece could be turned around and back out the door by the end of next week, and she made a mental note to call Elsie. The call would give Elsie the pleasure of letting Ginny Mae know her mama's Depression glass would soon have a new home. And she imagined Elsie would make the most of an opportunity to pass on suggestions about arranging and dusting it.

Mona turned in at every garage sale they passed, picking up odds and ends of pottery and glassware and a small pine bookcase for her office. But the prize of the morning was a die-cast replica of a Harley Fat Boy for a dollar. She managed to pay for it and slip it into her purse without Hallie noticing. It seemed like the perfect surprise, something to mark their time together.

If she was lucky, it might take the sting out of the news of the call. Mona knew she had to tell Hallie her parents were coming in ten days, but she didn't dare guess how Hallie might react. A tantrum seemed likely, or maybe a stony silence. Mona suddenly wondered where the key to the Harley had ended up.

A hand-lettered sign on an open stretch of farm country indicated an estate sale, and Mona turned north. Hallie had unscrewed the cap on a bottle of water Mona had thrown into a battered blue cooler she always kept in the truck, and she offered Mona a drink. Hallie was draining the last drops when they pulled up to a yellow, two-story clapboard at the end of a winding drive lined by towering pines. The "Centennial Farm" sign indicated that the property had been in family hands for at least a hundred years, and Mona practically leaped from the truck in anticipation of rooms stacked with family treasures.

She'd tagged a bargain-priced mission-style rocker and walnut dresser in the front parlor before she realized Hallie hadn't followed her. *The girl needs space,* Mona told herself as she eyed a collection of aged metal toys in a corner hutch. *Time just to be.* It was one reason she'd stuffed a wad of towels and a bottle of sunscreen behind the truck seat—in case a beach shouted out their names, and they were forced to answer. Or in case a sunset called, and they needed a cozy place to sit.

Mona wandered the rooms as long as the nagging awareness of Hallie's absence allowed her, checking her Timex every five minutes. Twenty minutes had passed before she gave herself permission to go looking, and she headed up the stairs.

She found her niece in a tiny upstairs bedroom, collapsed on a wooden rocker in front of an open window. A fan was wedged between the sill and the sash, wafting heavy, humid air into the room. The walls were papered in garish red-flocked paper, and a red-braided cord was nailed across the doorway leading to the hall. Mona slipped under the cord, plopped her huge leather purse to the floor, and leaned back against the doorframe.

"Looks like you're ready for lunch. Your old aunt wearing you out?"

"Hardly. I just needed air."

Hallie's T-shirt was sticking to her chest, and Mona watched as she pulled it away from her stomach and fluffed it.

"I'm probably not supposed to be in here, am I? I figured the rope was there to let people know this stuff wasn't for sale, but I'd give fifty bucks for this fan right about now."

Mona smiled. "And would that be fifty bucks of your own money, or money you stole from your mom?"

Hallie stuck her tongue out.

"You're not spending a dime, girl, here or any-place else. In fact, you're my slave until your parents come for you. Five bucks an hour for whatever I can make you do that I don't feel like doing. And right now that means loading furniture."

Hallie groaned, stretched her legs, and rose. "Who needs air anyway? Breathing is highly overrated." She laughed, then sobered. "Aunt Mona? It was just a joke, the breathing thing."

But Mona wasn't listening. She stared past Hallie and walked slowly across the faded Oriental rug, stopping just inches from the rocker where she'd been sitting.

"Aunt Mona? Are you all right?"

Mona felt the brush of her niece's hand on her arm, and she found her voice.

"You've been sitting in my mother's chair, Hallie. I can't believe it."

Mona leaned down and brushed her fingers over the pressed-back pattern of the oak rocker. Her eyes searched every line, every detail.

"This is impossible. This chair is new, and my mother's was over a hundred years old."

She knelt and examined the rope carving on the legs and stretchers, then ran her hand along the underside of the seat. Her eyes searched for the signatures of childhood. Tooth marks in the gentle curve of the right armrest, scratches and scars on the varnished seat, but she didn't find them.

"It's not really *her* chair, is it?" Hallie asked in disbelief. "I mean, it's just one that looks a lot like Gram's, right?"

Mona rose slowly to examine the design in the pressing that accented the center slat of the back. "No. I mean, yes. I'm not sure. I just know it's identical. Let me show you something."

Her eyes searched for more details as Hallie crossed the room and bent down. Mona took her hand and traced a design in the carving.

"If you look carefully, you can see the letters *H* and *S* carved into the scrollwork. You'd have to be told they were there to find them. Those are my grandma's initials, Hilma Stone. My grandfather carved them when he made the chair for my grandmother. This is an exact reproduction of my mother's chair. Which means someone out there has the actual chair and is copying it to sell. Which means I could find it."

Hallie was silent for a moment, as if absorbing the words. "You're not kidding?"

Mona stroked the wood softly. "Of course I'm not kidding." She turned to look at her niece. "Why would I kid about something like that?"

Mona saw a shadow of anger flicker across Hallie's face. "I don't know. Because random things don't happen like this. You probably rigged this whole deal up to impress me with some kind of spiritual point or something. Some dumb kind of object lesson for me, like when I was a kid." Hallie inched slowly backward toward the door as she spoke.

Mona laughed. "It's you who's got to be kidding, girl. You're the one who ran away from home yesterday, if I recall, sending me gallivanting halfway across the state to find you. Do you really think I had the brains to think this up last night, then call someone early this morning, ask them to whip up a reproduction of my mother's chair that I would give my spleen and kidneys to own myself, I might add, and then arrange for them to put it in a roped-off room so that you could just happen to find it and sit in it while I was downstairs? You're totally nuts."

Hallie had slipped beneath the roping and out into the hall, and Mona resisted the urge to follow her.

"Well, this is just too darn creepy for my taste. I think I'll get that loading started." She turned and headed for the stairs. "And why the heck would any sane mother name her kid Hilma?" she hollered over her shoulder.

Mona watched the red curls disappear down the stairwell. Then she reached for her purse and dug out a Polaroid camera, measuring tape, notebook, and pen. A few minutes later she emerged from the bedroom with measurements, a picture, and a written description of every detail of the chair.

It took Mona only five annoying minutes to get the answers she needed from the estate-sale manager, a tall, slender woman with an aloof business presence and silver reading glasses dangling from a delicate chain.

No, the chair was not for sale, a family member from out of state had inherited it as part of the estate and was keeping it. Yes, she was willing to call them and make a generous offer. No, she did not know where the chair had been acquired, but she believed it was from a local dealer. No, she was not willing to give out the name and number of the estate executors or family members, but she would be willing to take Mona's name and number to pass on to them.

Ten miles down the road, Mona realized she'd forgotten to purchase the mission rocker and walnut dresser, but it only made matters easier in the end. All Hallie had seemed interested in loading into the truck was herself, and she hadn't been able to do that fast enough.

Mona was content to let the silence swirl through the cab as they made their way to a downtown café in Newaygo. Heaven knew she didn't lack for things to think about as Hallie leaned back against the sticky vinyl and pretended to sleep. They found a booth in a corner of a knotty-pine-paneled diner where Mona distractedly watched a sullen Hallie toy with her food. Her own salad was wilted, and it appeared that the waitress had dumped an entire bottle of Thousand Island in a pool in the center.

It was a long, silent lunch, and Mona was eyeing the dessert menu for signs of chocolate when Elsie called. It took Mona four rings to find the cell phone in her purse.

"And whatever happened to common courtesy, I'd like to know? Harold and me been waitin' for your call, girl."

"I was just getting ready to dial your number."

"Don't waste my time makin' up excuses for yourself. Now how's that child?"

"Great. We're just enjoying a bite of lunch and stimulating conversation."

Hallie glared from across the table where she was busy shredding her napkin and rolling it into tiny balls.

"Needs the Lord, that one, no two ways about it. You can only run so far from Him, you know. I'm just glad she's all right."

Mona nodded, knowing Elsie wouldn't wait for a response.

"Well, honey, I thought I should give you an update from here. Gotta big sale this morning. That claw-foot dining-room table and four chairs. And not a word of hagglin' on the price. And Sharon Wendel did finally come in and pick up both of those copper boilers. I gave her a few suggestions for clearin' out the clutter in her parlor, but I don't think she listened to a word. Gotta little touch of 'tude, that one."

"And I supposed you shared your opinions about her 'tude with her?" Mona asked dryly as she stabbed at a soggy lettuce leaf.

"Now don't you get sassy with me. Harold and I hain't done too bad here with you gone and him with a busted foot 'n' all."

"No! You mean he broke it?"

Hallie looked interested for the first time since Mona had answered the call.

"Just badly bruised, Doc Prentice said. But I'm takin' good care of him. He's in his recliner with Oscar in the back room with his foot up, and I'm bringing him tea. And I had Jessica bake him his own lemon cake. Doc says he'll be better in a splickety second."

"Let me tell Hal what's going on, Elsie." Mona pulled the phone away and repeated Harold's prognosis as Hallie took her first bite of nachos.

"I can come home if you need me, Elsie," Mona spoke back into the phone. "I'll bring Hallie with me, and she can meet all of you. She barely had time to say hello when she came for the grand opening." Mona crammed a quick bite of drippy salad into her mouth.

"No need. Things here are smooth as a school-marm's legs. Oscar's doing just fine. Took him and Tessa over to Jessica's so's they could play with the grandkids for a few days. I figure a few days with Jessica's kids might slim that pup down a notch or two. Gettin' fat, that one."

Mona figured it was safe to take another bite or two before Elsie took a breath.

"And I saved the best for last. Some rich couple on their way from Traverse City headin' down to Detroit scooped up that gorgeous mahogany reproduction piecrust table you picked up from Elmer Dean. Told me they want another one in two weeks when they come through again to give to their daughter for an anniversary present."

Mona swallowed and laid down her fork. "That's wonderful, Elsie. I guess I need to leave more often. I hardly know what to say."

"Praise the Lord would do for starts. I saw that

letter from Eskel Barkel. Mind you, I wasn't tryin' to read it, but I saw it when I was cleanin' up the office a bit. You think about sellin' this place to that man, and you'll have some business to do with Harold 'n' me."

"I'm not selling."

Hallie's eyes flickered to her aunt's face once again.

"God put you in this shop for a reason, and just because things been a little thin lately doesn't mean you run."

"I'm not running."

"You best not be, or what will you be teachin' that child there? You worked out a good business plan and budget, and you've been stickin' to it. We got two new shops comin' in downtown in the next six months, and the city council's talkin' about smartin' things up a bit with new lampposts and flowerpots. You just hold on, girl. I told Harold I'd set you straight.

"Now that we got that settled, I need you to swing over to Elmer Dean's shop near Ludington and pick up another piecrust table. I s'pose you got the checkbook?"

"Yes, I have the checkbook."

"They want exactly the one they bought today. Same size, same stain, same design."

"Got it. And Elsie, I've got something for you to do, too. Call Ginny Mae and tell her I've picked up that sideboard. I'll be running it back to town in a day or two, and she can come by and take a look at it. If it's what she's looking for, she can be arranging her mother's china within a week."

"Like I said, girl, praise the Lord. He's watchin' out for you."

Mona thought of the chair. She opened her mouth, then closed it as she glanced at Hallie, who was placing droplets of water on her placemat in a random pattern. Now was not the time to tell Elsie about her grandmother's chair. She was sure to ask questions there weren't any answers for. Yet.

"I know He is."

A moment later, Mona hung up. The shop had seen its best day of sales since opening week, and Hallie had finished her nachos.

Mona smiled. Who would have thought that a day that started with rotten hamburgers and dead bugs could change so suddenly?

Chapter Eight

It had seemed like a good decision at the time, but now Adam Dean wasn't so sure. He glanced in the rearview mirror at the lathe strapped down in the back of his dark blue Suburban. Five hundred bucks was a lot of cash for a piece of used wood-working equipment, even if his tools were his bread and butter. But he'd had little choice when the one his father had passed on to him had finally given up the ghost. The Findleys were expecting their entertainment unit to be installed in their media room by the end of the week, and the last thing he needed was for them to cancel the project and leave him with a custom built-in to unload in his uncle's shop.

Adam glanced at his watch. Three thirty. He'd promised Sadie he'd be back to close up by four so she wouldn't be late for her date. Ben Somebody-or-Other. Adam couldn't be totally sure who Sadie's Guy of the Month was for June. There had been a Sam, he was sure, followed by a Jason or Jared. And those were only the ones she let them know about. He just knew if she were his daughter, he'd be pulling out his hair.

Lucky for her—for them all, really—his cousin Steph had had the resources of the entire Dean family at her disposal for raising her daughter these past sixteen years. Uncle Elmer and Aunt Florence and the aunts and uncles on both sides had risen to the occasion with English stoicism and pledged support for the unwed mother. And over the years, Sadie had given Steph plenty of opportunities to tap into the combined wisdom of an extended family.

Traffic was slow on the winding two-lane. Ahead of him, at least a dozen cars were trailing behind a station wagon pulling a fishing boat. Adam checked his speedometer. Thirty-seven. The winding road between Ludington and Applington didn't afford many opportunities for passing, and he knew he'd simply have to wait it out. If he got lucky, the station wagon would turn north in the direction of one of the area lakes, and he could get back to the shop before Sadie headed out the door.

Not that he had any exciting prospects for a Saturday night. The standing invitation to play Uno with Uncle Elmer and Aunt Florence held as much appeal as a root canal. The day had been frustrating enough with the lathe dying and the trip to Eskel Barkel's to pick up a used one. He'd never cared much for Eskel. Not that he knew him well, but the man was just a bit too pushy, in Adam's opinion. The kind of eager enthusiasm that always made Adam think of a late-night infomercial salesman. Since Adam had come to work for Uncle Elmer, Eskel had made frequent offers to hire him to work for Reinbeck's Reproductions. A good salary and benefits. Room for advancement with a national chain. The opportunity to move out of his uncle's guest house. Every time Adam came face-to-face with Eskel, the offer was made again, and every time his answer was a quiet no.

He wasn't sure exactly why; he just knew it wasn't time. The timing always had to be right, especially in the big things, usually in the small things.

When he'd married Julie, he'd been sure, not just about her, but about why he couldn't live without her. And when they'd moved to live near her parents, neither one of them had known why, but they both believed it was right. The day came when Julie was diagnosed with cancer, and the reason had become clear, the reason that had been there long before they'd known it.

When Julie had died and Uncle Elmer called to ask Adam to help with the business, he knew it was right once again.

"It would mean a lot for us to have you here, Adam. Your aunt Florence hasn't been quite herself lately, and you here would mean I could spend more time with her, fuss over her a bit. And your cousin Steph would welcome the chance for Sadie to have a bit more influence from a godly man. Heaven knows, that child is giving her mother a run for her money."

And for now, Adam was sure once again. The answer for Eskel Barkel was clear. Wait.

A short distance ahead, the station wagon was signaling for a right-hand turn, and for a moment, Adam envisioned getting back to the shop before four after all. The car and trailer turned to the right, and the red Grand Am that had been riding the boat's tail shot forward. The trail of cars followed suit, jockeying for position as the road fanned out into a slow lane and passing lane up a steep mile rise. Locals knew it was the only opportunity to pass on the curving road for the next thirty miles. Adam checked his rearview mirror and pulled into the slower right-hand lane.

The truck behind him remained in the passing lane, and he could hear the low thrum of the engine as the vehicle attempted to accelerate to pass. Within seconds he realized that the slow lane would end before the truck would gain enough momentum to pull past him. Instinctively, he eased up on the gas and the truck pulled beside the Suburban. He glanced to his left and saw a teenage girl with her feet propped on the front dashboard, a mane of red curls clutched in her right hand. She stared straight ahead, oblivious to his gaze, and apparently angry at someone. For a moment, he thought he recognized her, but he didn't cross paths with teenage girls often these days, except for a few gothic waifs who drifted in and out of the shop to talk to Sadie, and he was certain he would have remembered the owner of that startling hair if he'd ever met her.

The truck crept slowly past, nearly running him off the road as the lanes merged at the top of the hill. It was then that Adam saw the lettering on the rear door: "Stewartville Antiques, Treasures from the Past to Cherish for Tomorrow." He laughed and adjusted his sunglasses. Obviously the red-headed dealer from Stewartville so dead-set on the oak sideboard had a daughter. From the looks of her, she was a carbon copy of her mother, right down to the sour attitude.

It was then that Adam's right front tire blew,

and he realized that what had started as simply a bad day was headed straight into the Dumpster.

Mona was frustrated. The teenager with jet-black bobbed hair behind the counter obviously didn't know the first thing about antiques in general or Elmer Dean's shop in particular. And she knew even less about manners.

"You're telling me I can't place an order." It came out as more a statement than a question in a tone Mona didn't use often but used well. The skinny girl behind the counter seemed unimpressed.

"Of course you can place an order. I just don't know how to take one." The gaunt child in black jeans and a black T-shirt accented with artfully placed rips and tears blew on her freshly completed ebony manicure. The showroom was filled with the overpowering odor of nail polish, made even more pungent by the humidity and heat. Mona felt a headache coming on fast.

"Well, how can I place one if you don't know how to take one?"

"I guess you've got me there."

Hallie rolled her eyes. "Been sniffing that nail polish a little too long, honey?"

"Hallie!" Mona smiled in embarrassment as the girl behind the counter cocked her head to one side and met Hallie's direct stare.

"She's sorry for being so rude."

117

"Am not."

The girls continued their stare down.

"Are you sure no one else is available to answer my questions?" Mona glanced around the cabin's knotty-pine interior and tastefully arranged groupings of antique reproductions as she silently pleaded for someone to appear from somewhere.

"Just me, so I guess we'll just have to make it work, won't we? And did I tell you we close in five minutes?" The girl tore her gaze away from Hallie and gave Mona a saccharine smile. Mona smiled back with what she hoped was her most winsome look.

"Hallie, why don't you help me out here and take a look around the shop and see if you can find some wall shelving in cherry or mahogany for a gift for your mother and father. They've asked me to look for something for their study. And this young lady and I—I'm sorry, I'm sure I didn't catch your name . . ."

"Sadie, as if you actually give a rip."

Mona chose to ignore the comment.

"And Sadie and I will take care of ordering that piecrust table. I forgot to ask, do you work on commission?"

Hallie threw Mona a disgusted look and strode off to the front of the shop where several small wall shelves were grouped.

Mona hefted her purse from her shoulder and set

it carefully on the counter as she rummaged through its contents.

"I do believe, Sadie, that it might be best if I just left a note for Mr. Elmer Dean. Do you think that you could see that it gets to him?" She withdrew a small spiral notebook and pen. "It's rather important to me. I have an order to fulfill within two weeks, and the customer specifically requested one of your pieces."

Sadie tucked her arms across her bony chest. "Maybe, maybe not. Depends on whether or not I can come up with enough working brain cells. You know, the nail polish and all." She glanced in Hallie's direction, but Hallie continued her scrutiny of the wall shelving.

Mona smiled. "I've heard that the scent of money sometimes revives brain cells. How does five bucks sound?"

Sadie paused for a moment and glanced from Mona to Hallie and then back again. "She your daughter?"

Mona tried not to sound annoyed at the change of subject. "No. My niece."

"You taking care of her?"

For the second time that day, Mona counted to five. "Yes. For a time."

"How long?"

Hallie turned and faced the two of them. "Yeah, how long? Not that it's any of her business."

Mona searched for the right words. "For as long

119

as I can convince her parents to let her stay with me."

Hallie turned back to her examination of shelving.

Sadie slapped a legal pad on the counter. "That notebook of yours is too small. Uncle Elmer can't read small writing. And I don't accept bribes."

Mona tried not to look embarrassed.

"So you gonna get started on that note so I can get outta here on time?"

It took Mona a full five minutes to compose the note while Sadie alternated between tapping her foot and rolling her eyes. Elmer had supplied the original piecrust table, and it had been custom-made by one of his craftsmen. Mona gave every detail for ordering an identical piece, including dimensions, design, finish, and her requested date of delivery. Beneath the ordering information, she included a description of her grandmother's rocker and a request that Elmer contact her should he ever come across one like it. The note explained briefly that she was searching for a cherished family possession that had been lost to her and then concluded with her name and the phone numbers of the shop and her cell phone.

The clock behind the counter read 4:06 when Mona finished. Sadie had disappeared through a chintz curtain into a back room, and somewhere in the rear of the shop a door slammed. Mona hoped desperately that the girl hadn't simply walked off because it was closing time. She rang a silver bell on the counter as she neatly folded the yellow paper.

Within seconds, the chintz curtain parted and Sadie reappeared, slathering her lips with a glittery gloss. Mona handed her the note.

"If I could have just one more minute of your time, I'd like to explain something." She tried to hide the urgency in her voice. "I've included some information about a chair I'm looking for. It has nothing to do with the piecrust table, really, but someone in the area is doing reproductions of this chair, and I'd really like to find that person. The chair belonged to my mother and my grandmother, and it has the letters *H* and *S* carved into the pressed back at the top. I can even send a picture in a day or two if it would help. This chair really means a lot to me, and if your grandfather has any information at all about it, I'd be very grateful if he'd call me."

Mona stood silently as the girl surveyed her face with a steady gaze.

"I'll make sure he gets the note, but you should call him yourself about the table on Monday. I've been known to forget things sometimes. Now I really gotta be somewhere, and I need to lock up."

Mona managed to get out three thank-yous before she and Hallie were pushed out the front door. For a moment, she stood awkwardly on the front landing as she heard the door bolt fall into place behind them. Then with quiet resolve, Mona directed Hallie toward the truck and fell into step beside her.

Adam stood near the curtain that divided the back room of his uncle's shop from the showroom and listened as Sadie's footsteps skittered back toward the register. He heard the *ping* of the cash drawer opening and pulled the curtain aside just in time to see her slipping her hand into the pocket of her jeans.

"Just getting things closed up, I see."

"Yeah."

Adam stepped through the curtain and over to the counter. A glance at the cash drawer showed him it had been a slow afternoon. A half-dozen checks, about a hundred in twenties, another hundred in smaller bills. He glanced back toward Sadie. Her eyes stared straight into his.

"So what are you going to do about it?" she said.

"About what?"

"About what you think I just shoved in my pocket. About the fact you think I just ripped your uncle off again. About the fact you don't trust me as far as you can spit. How's that for starters?"

Adam raised his eyebrows and crossed his arms.

"Seems like a pretty good list for starters."

"So?"

"I guess that would be my question for you. So?"

"Why should I tell you anything? You won't believe me. I'm just a liar and a thief to you, to all of you!"

Adam raised his eyebrows once again.

"Sadie, you're the one who refuses to believe what this family has told you over and over again, and I'll say it again now. You're forgiven for what you did last summer, and if you'd take the time to think about it, you'd realize I've never brought it up to you. But if you want to be trusted again, you have to act like someone who can be trusted. That would mean honoring your mom's curfew and the rules she sets down for you. Oh, and not acting like a martyr for being in a family that's put themselves on the line because they give you a few rules to live by."

Adam uncrossed his arms and leaned against the counter as he watched for Sadie's reaction. Her gray eyes had turned cold. He could read the mistrust. He'd never understood what had put it there, but it seemed to be there for everyone in the family these days.

"So, if you want to say anything more to me, I'm here to listen, and if not, you're free to go and meet Whatever-His-Name-Is."

Her head tilted slightly. "So you're not going to make me turn my pockets inside out?"

"No. Not unless that's what you want to do."

There was a pause as her eyes searched his. "It's not."

She turned on her heel and swept through the curtain toward the back door. Adam heard it open with a metallic scrape.

"And for your information, I didn't take a dime!"

The door slammed.

Adam didn't know how long he stood in the silence before he moved. The room felt suddenly stifling, and Julie's face flashed before him. Did she know he was here with Uncle Elmer and Aunt Florence, whom she'd always adored? Did she know that, in his own awkward way, he was committing himself to family without her presence beside him? Did she know how hard it was to do it alone, day after day, to feel part of something yet not part of it? Did she know how he ached with missing her?

His head dropped. The only thing he knew some days was that his ache for her was so deep, he felt his very bones longed to cry out her name.

He blinked against the burning and blurring of his eyes as he spotted a yellow folded paper on the counter. The note from the woman he'd heard through the curtain talking to Sadie, he imagined. He opened it and scanned the lines once, then twice, as a quiet realization dawned. His eyes flickered to the signature.

Mona VanderMolen, Stewartville Antiques.

He walked slowly through the chintz curtains and pondered the note.

Mona VanderMolen. An antique dealer with flaming hair and a cookie-cutter daughter. Someone who cared about family enough to chase halfway across the state for her mother's chair. Someone whose passion for a family treasure had put a quaver in her voice that had passed through the chintz curtain and captured his attention on a day when just about everything else in his life was screaming to be noticed.

He tucked the carefully folded note into the top pocket of his chambray shirt. Then he slowly lowered his tall frame into a pressed-back oak chair with rope carvings.

Chapter Nine

By the time Mona pulled the box truck to the end of the lane, she was exhausted. The ride home had been a knot of silences and superficialities, and the sheer emotion of the past twenty-four hours had left her drained. It hadn't helped that the last thirty minutes of the drive had brought a deluge of rain that had obliterated the road and nearly sent them into a ditch. She managed to edge the truck close to the storage shed, wondering with every inch how she was ever going to back it out again without taking out a few sassafras bushes.

Before Mona killed the engine, Hallie had flung a beach towel over her head and raced up the path. By the time Mona reached the house, drenched and dripping, Hallie had curled up in a nest of blankets on the living room floor. Mona wasn't quite sure if her niece was sleeping, but she was sure that, sleeping or not, Hallie didn't want to be disturbed.

Mona's left arm was throbbing scarlet from the glaring sun that had poured through her open window all day, and her head was beginning to ache. Water streamed from her hair in rivulets that snaked down the back of her shorts. Somewhere in the back of her mind she could hear Elsie's voice scolding her for not using sunscreen or taking an umbrella. She decided it was evidence of God's grace that Elsie was not there at that moment.

She contemplated pouring an iced tea and dropping onto the couch, but hunger drove her to the kitchen. They hadn't eaten for hours, and her usual stash of chocolate had run out somewhere between Montague and Whitehall. She dragged a barstool to the sink and busied herself slicing watermelon and shucking the sweet corn she'd bought at a roadside stand.

Through the front windows, she watched the torrent outside. Beyond the embrace of the house, the storm roared. A gripping magnetism had energized Lake Michigan, a palpable force that blackened the churning water. The surf towered in thunderous cascades of foam that clawed at the beach and receded in angry swaths as

Mona watched Hallie sleep. Her hands tore at the husks, then gently pulled the strands of tassel until each ear of corn lay stripped clean, ready for the boiling water. She poured herself a cup of steaming tea and leaned back on the stool, watching the mound of blankets for signs of movement. For a long while, the only sound was the fury of the storm and the gentle bubbling of the pot.

Then the nest of blankets stirred, and a muffled voice spoke.

"How long?"

Mona turned and slowly dropped the corn into the rolling water. "Fourth of July. Ten days."

"Really? And you actually believe they'll keep their word?"

"I'm choosing to."

Mona scanned the pile of blankets, but Hallie's head remained buried in a red afghan.

"And then what?" Hallie asked.

Mona wiped her hands on the legs of her shorts and stood up. She walked to the scarlet pile and sat down cross-legged beside it. "I don't know. What do you want the answer to be?"

"You think I know the answer?"

"What did you want when you came?"

Mona watched the fingers clutching the edge of the blanket tighten their grip. "For the nightmares to stop. To stop hating myself." Hallie's voice was a whisper.

Mona bowed her head close to the blanket and stroked the fingers.

"To start forgiving yourself. That comes first. Sometimes it comes in bits and pieces every day for a long time. Do you want that? Do you think it's possible?"

"No."

"If you don't think it's possible, why did you come?"

The fingers drew the blanket tightly over her head. "I don't know! Just because . . . I had to!"

"Of course. You had to, even though you don't know why. It makes a lot of sense."

The covers flew back, and anger shot from Hallie's eyes. For a moment, Mona saw Ellen staring back at her.

"Stop mocking me! You sound just like my mother!"

Mona lowered her voice. "Have I ever mocked you, Hallie Bowen? Ever? And would I choose now to be the first time? I think what you said makes a lot of sense because I think you came here for a reason, a reason you don't understand. I think you had to come because something bigger than your heart and your mind brought you here. I believe God brought you here, kicking and screaming, in spite of yourself."

"That's the stupidest thing I ever heard. I hate when you talk like this, all your stupid God junk."

Anger was coursing from Hallie's eyes, but there were no tears.

"Why?" Mona smoothed Hallie's face with the palm of her hand.

"Because He's not there. Your God isn't there!" Hallie pounded her fists into the blankets. "You want me to believe in someone who let my sister die. You want me to trust a God like that?" Her body was shaking with sobs, and Mona ached to gather her in her arms, but she waited until the tremors slowed.

"And I suppose you got angry with Santa Claus because he didn't bring you any presents this year. Of course you didn't, because you don't believe in him. We only waste our anger on people we believe are real. And you're angry at God."

"The God you're talking about and the God I see aren't the same person."

"Hallie, do you remember when the Smithers down the street lost their two-year-old daughter to pneumonia?"

"Yes."

"When they lost their baby, did you doubt God the same way you've doubted Him since Stacy died?"

Hallie blinked and picked at the blanket. "Of course not. I hardly knew the Smithers."

"And when Grandpa and Grandma VanderMolen died, did it hurt you the same way Stacy's death hurts?"

"I . . . it . . . it wasn't the same. They were old, and Mom and Dad didn't bring us to see them that much. I mean, I felt bad, but jeez, Aunt Mona, you're making me sound like a crappy granddaughter."

"No, Hallie, you don't sound crappy, you sound honest. So God wasn't being unfair when the Smithers' baby died because you didn't know the family very well, and God wasn't being unfair when Grandpa and Grandma VanderMolen, died because they were old, but suddenly God isn't fair when something bad happens that hurts *you* a lot?"

"I hate you. Don't talk to me like this."

"I'm sure we'll both get over it. You hate me for making you think, but that's what you wanted when you came. A chance to think, to figure it out."

Hallie sat up and pounded her fists in her lap.

"Your God is a monster! Yes, He hurt me, but He hurts millions of people every day. He lets there be wars and babies who die of cancer and parents who abuse their kids and people who starve and giant waves that wipe people off the planet! And you want me to believe He's a God who cares?"

"So He's responsible for all the bad stuff in your world and in the universe. It's His job to fix all the bad stuff. Is that it? Wars, abuse, death, suffering. You don't want any of it in your world, right? He's supposed to give us a perfect world and everything we need. Well, news flash, He did that once and we screwed it up, and this is what we got.

"And what about the good stuff? People cured of cancer and people saved from starvation? People who give up their lives to help the suffering? What about bodies and hearts that heal and a planet that gives us food and air? What about sunsets and the northern lights? This God you don't believe in, the God you're so angry with, is He in any of the beautiful and mysterious things in your world?"

"I can't believe what you believe." Hallie's sobbing had stopped, and Mona took her hand.

"You don't even know what you believe, because the pain is the only thing you've let yourself see and hear for two years. I want you to see a God who doesn't cause our pain or even erase our pain but bears our pain."

"He's the cause of my pain."

"Actually, Hallie, we're the cause of *His* pain. Maybe that's one reason He understands us so well. In our hearts, we all measure God by how we think He's managing our little piece of the world. But His plan is bigger than that. He's bigger than that. I think His plan is bigger than just whether your sister and my niece drowned. I think it takes in the whole universe and beyond. He lets me see glimpses of it, but only glimpses, and I'd miss them entirely if I wasn't looking and didn't believe they were there."

Hallie's breathing had slowed to a gentle rhythm, and Mona stroked her arm.

"When you made the decision to run away, you knew I'd come find you, didn't you? You knew nothing would keep me from tracking you down until I knew you were safe, right?"

"Yes."

"And you knew your mother and father would do the same thing?"

Mona waited, but Hallie was silent.

"Just be still, girl. God's coming. He's tracking you down until He knows you're safe."

Hallie bit her lower lip and stared at her hands. They sat in silence for a few moments while Mona weighed her thoughts. She knew her next words would be hard, and she wanted to be sure of them. She lifted her niece's chin until their eyes met.

"I want to tell you something. I want to tell you about my nightmare."

"Your nightmare?"

Mona saw the confusion and nodded.

"Yes, the one I've had since Stacy died. It used to come a lot. Now it's just every once in a while."

"Your nightmare? A real one, not one you're making up?"

"Nope. I'm not creative enough for this one. Gram VanderMolen bobbing around Lake Michigan in a flowerpot."

"You're jerking me around."

"No jerking, but I am a little embarrassed. Shrinks everywhere would have a heyday with me. So it goes like this . . ."

Mona scooted closer to Hallie so they were sitting face-to-face as she tucked the afghan around both their legs.

"I'm standing in Lake Michigan at some beach—I don't know which one. For some reason, I'm wearing Gram VanderMolen's pink robe."

"The one hanging on your bedroom door, the one you always wear when you're here?"

"I had it on last night."

"And it's frightening. Kind of nursing-home chic."

"So are you going to be quiet and listen, or what? I haven't told anybody about this dream, so at least pretend to appreciate the effort." Mona wondered if Hallie could read in her eyes how true the admission was.

Hallie fluffed the covers like a child settling in for a bedtime story, and Mona felt her lean against her arm as she nestled in. It was all she wanted.

"So I'm standing in the lake, wading in the water. There's a voice calling me from the shore, but I don't look, and I don't know who it is. I see Gram VanderMolen bobbing along in the water in a flowerpot, crocheting for all she's worth, a red afghan, this afghan, I think. There are lights flashing behind me and the voice is louder, but I

133

still don't turn. Gram looks up. She smiles at me, and she winks, and then she's gone. I suddenly hear sirens, and I'm facing the shore. Three ambulances are all lined up there, and Grandpa VanderMolen is calling something to me, but I can't hear him over the sirens. The robe is all wet and pulling at my legs, and I feel like I'm going to go under, but I'm facing out into the lake again. And you and Stacy are there floating on a yellow air mattress. And then . . . and then . . . Stacy slips off the mattress and disappears."

Mona counted to five as she waited for Hallie's response. Then another five, and another.

"You're psycho."

Mona laughed, and relief seeped into her bones and her spirit eased.

"I prefer the word *eccentric.* What teenage girl wouldn't want to have an eccentric spinster aunt?" Mona slipped her arm around Hallie's shoulders and drew her close. "And are you psycho, too? Can you talk about your dream? You know I won't make you if you don't want to."

Hallie threw her head back. "Ha! That's the scary thing about you. You're the only person who could ever make me do anything. So I want you to know that when I can talk about it, I'll tell you."

"Promise?"

"Promise. But I need you to tell me one more thing."

"Anything."

"Does your dream scare you?"

"Not anymore."

"When did it stop?"

The memory was starkly clear in Mona's memory, more clear even than the day Stacy had died.

"About six weeks after the funeral. It was the same day I decided to leave teaching and close up the beach house for a while. I got up early that morning, before the sun rose. I prayed for a while on the deck—I don't know how long. Then I just walked into the water with my clothes on and floated on my back. I stayed there until the stars faded into daylight. It was like saying good-bye and moving on. It helped me feel like I wasn't leaving her behind. It's like God allowed me to shed the guilt inside myself that I'd been trying to claw off on my own."

"So after that, the nightmare didn't scare you?"

"Not so much. It helped me, Hal, because it was the day I decided to trust something bigger than my pain. I'd be lying if I told you there were days when I didn't struggle with guilt and the horror of losing Stacy. But pain always drives us toward God or away from Him, and I've allowed it to drive me toward Him. That's been a precious thing to me."

From the direction of the kitchen, an acrid odor caught Mona's attention.

"The corn! I've boiled the corn dry."

She leaped from the floor and sprinted to the kitchen, hollering over her shoulder. "And don't pretend to be surprised. You wouldn't be eating at my house if dinner wasn't served at the sound of the smoke alarm."

They ate in the loft that evening at Hallie's request, an unspoken ceremony. Mona climbed up the ladder first, Hallie handing up glasses of iced tea, bowls of watermelon, and plates of seared sweet corn.

After they'd eaten, Mona made a nest of pillows and blankets in a corner of the loft, and they watched out the small window near the eaves as the storm raged over the lake. Their conversation slowly faded, and in the silence, Mona was grateful for things she could see, for the things she still couldn't shape into words, for the child beside her who clutched her sister's Mickey Mouse pillow in her arms. She knew that sometimes words were not needed, and silence was more than enough.

Chapter Ten

Mona tried not to smile. She knew it was one of many things that irritated the dickens out of Hallie when they argued, and an argument was not on her list of priorities for the day.

"You can't expect me to go to church this

morning! For heaven's sake, I packed in a saddlebag, and all I've got are T-shirts and jeans."

Mona poured Cocoa Krispies into two large, stoneware bowls and pretended to ignore her. Her mother's terry bathrobe was tied at the waist, and her feet were bare. Her chin-length hair was still wet from the shower, and she expected it to be another major frizz day.

"Then we're even, I guess. My duffel bag offers an assortment of unmatching shoes, two shirts with stains of unknown origin, a pair of kneeless jeans, and a rawhide chew bone. But I have a plan. Let's pretend we're twins and deck ourselves out in cotton sarongs I have hanging in my closet, compliments of my Bahamas vacation. We could even stick flowers in our hair. Or we could both wear our leather biker clothes and see if that gets us any attention."

"Be serious. I'm not going to walk over there and make a fool of myself." Hallie slammed a spoon into her cereal, splashing milk onto the counter.

Mona chose to ignore it. "I am perfectly serious. Gilead is a Bible conference center. People come there to vacation, and I've never noticed a single fashion cop on their staff. And if there was one, you know I'd make it my mission to try to annoy him. Or her. Let's not be sexist here." Mona settled onto a stool next to her niece and dunked her cereal into her milk with the bottom of her spoon.

Cereal had to be damp to be eaten. It was one of her rules.

For the next few minutes, Mona endured Hallie's best display ever of eye-rolling and whining. But an hour later, she had prevailed, and two sandal-toting redheads in sarongs and cotton blouses headed out the front door and up the beach toward the conference grounds, one with a silk daisy in her hair and one without.

Mona always enjoyed walking the beach, even if it was a familiar five-minute jaunt to Gilead. She crossed down to the water toward the moister, firmer sand nearer the breaking waves.

"Make it sing," Mona called over her shoulder to Hallie, who appeared to be making a political statement by walking several yards behind.

"I'm not a child, Aunt Mona!"

"No one said you were, Hallie, although you seem to be acting a lot like one this morning."

She stopped and ground the balls of her feet into the sand, twisting back and forth like a sixties sock hopper. The sand squeaked with each motion of her feet.

"Don't pretend you don't remember when I taught you how to do that, Hallie Bowen," Mona called. It was a vivid memory for her. The girls had been six and eight, and it was the first time Ellen had trusted her to keep them. She and Phil had run off to Vegas for a long weekend, and it turned out to be four days that changed all of their lives.

The girls had believed in childhood magic then, the magic they'd lost six summers later. They had stayed in the water for hours that day, finally coming out to eat gritty peanut butter sandwiches and sliced apples on the beach. They'd rinsed their sticky fingers in the shallows and were heading back to the beach house when Mona had shown them the magical singing sand, grinding her feet into the beach and twisting as the girls watched in delight. At sunset that first day, she'd explained how moister sand at just the right distance from the water made noise under friction. But even with a scientific explanation, the girls had not lost their sense of wonder.

Now, Mona wondered if Hallie remembered that day. She looked in her direction, but Hallie had turned around and was walking backward. Words formed in Mona's head, but she held her tongue.

Within minutes, they reached the Gilead pool and turned east away from the beach and up the twisting, narrow road leading to the hotel, Sweet Shoppe, and Tabernacle. The road was lined with quaint cottages, and to the right, a path wound up a steep dune to the Prayer Tower. Clusters of families, adults, and teenagers were making their way up the sand-strewn road toward the Tabernacle where the beach road opened into a wide expanse of grass.

The walk took barely ten minutes, and Mona

could hear Hallie muttering under her breath as they approached the crowd streaming into the rustic, open-beamed building through double sets of screen doors on three sides. She let Hallie choose a wooden bench near the back, adjacent to one of the screened windows encircling the building, and they took their seats. A half-dozen vocalists and musicians were lining up at microphones spaced across a platform flanked by an organ and a baby grand piano. A man who appeared to be in his twenties strummed a guitar softly and adjusted the tuning. Behind the group, the Gilead logo hung on a huge banner against the knotty pine wall: "Gilead, a Place of Balm, a Place of Blessing," emblazoned in red over a swoop of softly rolling golden dunes.

The music began, and in her peripheral vision, Mona saw Hallie pick up a song sheet lying on the pew beside her and finger it as the strains of two acoustic guitars drifted over the crowd. The taller of the two players hummed softly for a moment and then spoke.

"Ladies and gentlemen, listen for a moment as we sing this first song for you, the theme of Gilead Conference Center for the past sixty-three years. May these words speak to your heart as the Spirit of God ministers to you today."

The music hung in the air for a moment, and then the voices began:

There is a balm in Gilead to make the wounded whole;
There is a balm in Gilead to heal the sin-sick soul.
Sometimes I feel discouraged and think my work's in vain,
But then the Holy Spirit revives my soul again.

Mona tipped back her head and closed her eyes as the words washed over her. Then Hallie's voice broke through.

"I can't do this."

The congregation joined on the hymn as Mona slipped her arm around her niece's shoulder and inclined her head in her direction.

"You're not a hostage, my dear. Go or stay— it's your choice." She leaned back on the wood-slatted bench, withdrew her arm, and closed her eyes again. When she opened her eyes a few moments later, she found the music sheet folded in half on the seat beside her, and Hallie was gone.

Mona picked up the paper and ran her fingers up and down the crease for a moment. She'd decided much earlier that morning, on the beach alone and praying, that she wouldn't follow if Hallie left, and she wouldn't force her to go in the first place if she refused.

Last night she'd pushed enough. Today it was time to pray. She rose from the bench and walked back out of the Tabernacle, the music fading behind her.

Retracing their steps down the sidewalk leading to the lane to the beach, she walked as quickly as possible. When she reached the path to the Prayer Tower, she turned off the road and up the winding path. The sarong wasn't made for hiking, and it entangled her legs as she ascended the timbered steps built into the dune. She paused briefly on a landing to catch her breath as her eyes scanned the area for Hallie, but she was nowhere to be seen.

Mona didn't know whether to be relieved or concerned. She reminded herself again that she wasn't spying and that she wasn't following Hallie, even though Hallie would never believe it if she spotted her. And the last thing Mona wanted to risk was Hallie's trust.

The Prayer Tower, a boxy, wooden structure built on sturdy pylons that lifted it way up in the treetops high above the beach, had long been Mona's refuge, and she had always respected it for what it was—a place for those at Gilead to be alone with God. She had climbed the wooden stairs many times, but she hadn't remembered there being quite so many.

She reached the top of the dune and made her way along the wooden walkway leading to the tower. She hesitated outside the simple wood door, then quickly reached for the knob and stepped inside.

It was exactly as she'd remembered. The room was small, barely twelve-feet square, constructed of hewn timbers and pine planks. A hip roof rose above it, and large screen windows surrounded it on all four sides. The tower was embraced by massive jack pines, birches, sugar maples, and oaks. It was a place of solace, high above the busyness of the conference center below. The sound of the surf breaking on the shore wove its song through the leaves and surrounded the tower with its presence as Mona stood and listened.

Below, she could hear the sound of footsteps along one of the wooden walkways leading to the tower. Their rhythm moved closer, then stopped. Mona closed her eyes and drank in the musty scent of moss and decaying leaves. A wooden bench had been built into all four sides of the tower, and she chose the seat farthest from the door, where the ground fell away sharply with the slope of the dune. The Prayer Tower had always made her feel suspended somewhere between the earth and the sky, and she remembered that the girls had always loved it here.

Mona tipped her head back and closed her eyes once again and listened to the soft murmur of leaves rustling and waves stroking the shore. For a long time, she listened, and then the prayers came.

For healing, for balm, for revival. For Hallie, for Ellen and Phil, for herself. At times, her pleading was hedged by words. At other moments, her heart cry came with words that could not be uttered. When she finally opened her eyes and glanced at her watch, more than an hour had passed. She rose and opened the door to the walkway back down the dune.

Sitting beneath a huge oak on a knotted tangle of exposed roots was Dan Evans, facing the door, an open book in his hand. He rose quickly.

"I'm sorry. I didn't want to disturb you."

He wore khaki shorts and a navy polo shirt, and as he tucked the small leather book into his back pocket, he brushed sand from the seat of his shorts.

"I saw Hallie leave the Tabernacle, and I followed her just to make sure she was all right. She headed back to the beach house, and when I left her, she was sitting on the beach, staring at the water. She wasn't much in the mood for talking. Just some yelling about how I was stalking her."

"And you're surprised?"

Dan laughed. "Not a bit. I sat down next to her for a while just to annoy her and told her she wouldn't know what real friendship was if it smacked her upside the head. Then I smacked her upside the head. Gently, of course. Just to get a reaction."

"And I trust you weren't disappointed?"

"I lived to tell you about it. Guess I should consider myself lucky."

Mona crossed the few steps from the tower to where Dan stood. "I never took the opportunity to tell you how much it meant to have you looking out for Hallie. She can be quite a handful. You've been gracious and kind, and I'm not sure I can find the words to express my gratitude."

Dan shoved a hand into his pocket. "It's really no big deal. I'm glad she's here, and I'm glad to help. Helps keep me out of trouble."

It was Mona's turn to laugh. "Right. And what else have you been doing to keep yourself out of trouble for the past two years?"

"Guarding here at Gilead during the summer months. School in the winter months. Michigan State for veterinary medicine. Keeping an eye on Mom." He was silent for a moment before asking, "And what about Hallie?"

"Well, that would be seeing her counselors, failing classes, giving her parents grief, seeing more counselors, shaking her fist at God. Oh, and I almost forgot. Stealing a motorcycle and a wad of cash and running away."

"I'm sorry. I really am. I'd heard she was having a hard time, but I didn't know any of the particulars."

"A hard time, yes. An understatement. But back to you. What about next year?"

Dan's eyebrows rose slightly and then dropped. "Good question. I've come to somewhat of a cash-flow crisis. It looks like I'm going to have to drop out for a year to work. Probably at the Y teaching swimming classes. It kind of puts a kink in my plans, but it'll work out."

"And what plans would those be?"

"To graduate in four years, then find an organization to hook up with and head out to do veterinary medicine in a developing country."

"I don't think there are any 'kinks,' Dan, just pauses while we figure out what's coming next."

"And what about you, Miss V?"

"Pauses and prayers, Dan. That seems to be my life these days. With a little chocolate thrown in here and there. The shop seems to be making it at the moment. I'm hoping to take Hallie back to Stewartville for a day or two. I don't suppose you have a day or two free to tag along?"

"Afraid not. They seem to be short of lifeguards this summer, and I've got to make money while I have the chance." Dan glanced down the trail in the direction of the beach. "I've really got to be going. I just wanted you to know Hallie was okay."

Mona hugged him good-bye and thanked him again before she headed down the stairs. When she reached the beach and the house came into view, she realized that Hallie was no longer sitting in the sand. She had moved to the shallows and was wading, her sarong swirling gently around her legs and drifting with the waves.

Mona let her be and slipped into the house to fix

a lunch that would go uneaten. Perhaps Hallie knew what she needed best. To step into the water, with the glare of the sun on her head, the pull of the surf on her legs, and to be lost for a moment in the power of something greater than herself.

Chapter Eleven

The vintage Coca-Cola clock on the living-room wall read ten o'clock as Mona slid open the door to the front deck, a cup of iced coffee and a Krispy Kreme balanced on a red stoneware plate in one hand. She knew she should have changed into her clothes hours ago, but Elmer Dean wouldn't know she was lounging in her pj's and eating doughnuts on the other end of the telephone. She settled on the top step leading to the beach and pulled two packets of artificial sweetener and a cordless phone from the pocket of the pink robe.

Based on Hallie's track record, Mona knew the child wouldn't be up before noon unless she was threatened with a squirt gun of ice water, which was precisely what Mona planned to do after she'd savored her glazed doughnut and called Elmer Dean.

She drank in the solitude. The last few days with Hallie had been both mind-bending and emotionally draining. From one moment to the next, it was difficult to predict whether she would erupt in a shower of tears or stalk off in a sullen silence.

Monday had been a disaster. Mona could have been on another planet, for all Hallie seemed to notice. She'd spent most of the day sleeping in the loft, only slipping down the ladder occasionally to pick through the refrigerator. And when Dan had stopped by after supper to invite her to Gilead for beach volleyball, the answer had been an icy no. Then she'd turned on her heel and climbed back into the loft. Mona had been mortified, but Dan had been gracious. As soon as he'd left, Hallie had stalked out of the house to read on the beach until dusk.

After the sun had set, Mona slipped into the water. She'd felt Hallie's eyes watching her from the loft window as she lay on her back, tracing shapes into the water under the stars and silently praying. She didn't know how well Hallie had slept that night, but there had been no nightmares.

The Krispy Kreme was heavenly, and Mona savored her first bite, chasing it with the coffee Elsie claimed she always made too weak. Then she sucked her fingers with the enthusiasm of a child and reached into her pocket for Elmer's business card. She prayed silently that the wraith-child Sadie wouldn't pick up.

A man's voice answered just as Mona was sucking a clump of icing from her left thumb with a sound she instantly realized resembled a junior high kiss.

"Dean's Antiques and Reproductions. And one

more obscenity from you and I'll slam this receiver down."

Mona felt her face flush.

"That was certainly not an obscenity, it was a Krispy Kreme. I don't know if you've ever had one, but the glaze gets all over your fingers and—"

"Glaze?"

"Yes, and—"

"Is this a business call?"

"Well, actually, yes, but—"

"Are you trying to place an order for doughnuts?"

"Of course not, that's ridiculous."

"Forgive me for being ridiculous when I answer the phone and find a woman making sucking sounds in my ear."

For a moment Mona was speechless.

"Is this Elmer?"

"No, it is not."

"How lucky for him. And when might you expect him?"

"I'm not sure. Not in the foreseeable future. How unfortunate for those of us who are left to deal with the rudeness of select members of his clientele. And how unfortunate for him, because he is in the throes of passing some rather impressive kidney stones, and in all likelihood he will be shipped to Muskegon where they can blast them to smithereens with some kind of medical Howitzer."

"Lithotripsy."

"Is that some kind of foreign curse word? Because I can still slam this receiver down."

Mona sighed. "LITH–oh–trip–see. The medical procedure for breaking up kidney stones. And I don't curse, in English or any other language for that matter, even when people like you give me reason to."

There was a choking sound on the other end of the phone, and Mona decided to interpret it as an apology.

"Apology accepted. Now if you could do me a huge favor and pass along a message for me. My name is Mona VanderMolen of Stewartville Antiques. Elmer sold me a gorgeous mahogany piecrust table several months ago. A Smithsonian reproduction, quite stunning actually. I've sold it to a customer who would like an identical one made and delivered to my shop in Stewartville as soon as possible. This weekend, preferably."

The man had obviously found his voice. "Mona VanderMolen. Ah, yes. Do you have an account with us, Mrs. VanderMolen?"

"That would be *Miss* VanderMolen. And not exactly. Well, not yet. I do hope to establish an account soon, but I'm sure you can find a copy of my previous purchase order. It was a magnificent piece, Mr. . . ."

"I'm absolutely certain that it was. And you are extremely fortunate that we have another in stock.

It can take the artisan months to craft his pieces. I'm sure you know they don't just roll off an assembly line like other reproductions."

"Yes, I'm sure." Mona was eyeing the remainder of her Krispy Kreme. "You can find my business address in your files, and a check will be ready upon delivery. Just one more thing. I left a note with a girl named Sadie the other day regarding a chair I'm trying to track down. I found a reproduction of it at an estate sale in the area, and I'd like to locate the person who now owns the original. It belonged to my mother and my grandmother and has extreme sentimental value."

"So your mother sold her mother's chair, even though it had extreme sentimental value?"

Resentment ignited like a flame in Mona's chest. It was none of this man's business that her father had gotten rid of her mother's things three weeks after she died. She searched for words that wouldn't betray the insult she felt.

"She died of cancer. It was sold with the estate through rather unfortunate circumstances. Unfortunate to me, at least."

The phone went silent for a moment.

"Cancer. I'm sorry."

Mona couldn't tell if she read condescension or sincerity in his tone.

"I'll be certain to pass that information on, Miss VanderMolen. You never know who might know what. You'll be hearing from us about the exact time and date of the delivery."

As she hung up a moment later, Mona was certain she heard two final words whispered into the phone.

Apology accepted.

"He's persistent, if nothing else," Mona said to herself as she rinsed her hands in the kitchen sink. Grabbing a dish towel from the counter, she walked to the door, and swung it wide for Dan Evans. He was wearing khaki cargo shorts and a Detroit Red Wings jersey, and he kicked his sizable sandals onto the back porch before stepping inside.

"Afternoon, Miss V. I see you're hulling strawberries. You must have known I was coming."

"As a matter of fact, you're an answer to prayer, Dan. You can do me a big favor. Take that overstuffed pillow in the corner there and give it a good heave onto that pile of blankets in the loft. Maybe wrap this watermelon inside before you toss it."

Mona winked as she spoke and shoved Dan toward a king-size Tweety Bird pillow that Hallie had flung from the loft earlier that morning.

"Oscar the Grouch up there threw that thing at me this morning when I tried to wake her up. She didn't seem to respond positively to my ice-water squirt gun."

Mona smiled as a wad of red hair appeared at the edge of the loft.

"Child abuser! And to think you were a teacher, treating children like that. And why can't a girl get a little extra rest on her vacation?"

"Get your tail down here, Hallie Bowen. It's nearly one thirty in the afternoon, and I've been trying to drag you down since eleven."

"Yeah," Dan added. "The tournament starts in half an hour, and you're going to need at least that long to find your face in all that hair."

"Beauty tips from you?" Hallie spat back. "The man who apparently owns only one pair of shorts?"

Mona sighed, crossed her arms, and turned back toward the kitchen. "Get decent and get down here. And if you don't hurry, I'm going to feed your breakfast *and* lunch to Dan, including all the strawberries. There aren't that many left anyway. I discovered they taste especially good if you eat them with Hershey's Kisses."

Dan laughed and slid onto a barstool. He carried himself with an ease beyond his years, and his voice boomed as he spoke. "It's a double-elimination volleyball tournament, Miss V, and we should be finished around six. I thought I'd invite some of the kids down here for a bonfire afterward, if you don't mind playing hostess and letting us use your john. We'll each pitch in a few bucks for hotdogs, Coke, chips, and anything else.

I figured you'd be willing to trade Hallie for some fresh meat."

He ducked as a pillow shot past his head and landed in the kitchen sink with a clatter of pots and pans. Mona just shook her head.

"Aim's a little off, don't you think?" he called into the loft as Mona placed a Krispy Kreme on a paper napkin and slid it in front of him.

"And what makes you think for one second that I'm going to be dragged off to your stupid tournament?" A hairbrush dropped to the living-room floor, and Mona was certain she heard a mutter of profanity.

"Get a grip on your tongue, girl, or you're not going anywhere. I'll put your little hiney in my truck and make you scavenge antique shops with me, if you'd rather. If I were you, I'd make a quick apology before Dan decides you're more trouble than you're worth."

Mona popped a few strawberries into her mouth for effect, just in case Hallie was looking.

"Oh, for heaven's sake. All right then, I'll go!" Two legs straddled the top of the ladder, and Hallie slid to the living-room floor like a firefighter on a call. Her red hair still stuck out in stray clumps, and her yellow T-shirt and denim shorts were wrinkled. She threw herself onto the other barstool and stuck her tongue out.

"I never was one to argue when it came to food. You're just lucky I'm starved."

Mona didn't scavenge through any antique shops. Instead, she threw herself and her mammoth purse into the box truck and headed to Meijer's, the gargantuan grocery store she'd missed so much in Stewartville. With the cash Dan had collected from the other kids, she loaded up on hotdogs, Coke, chips, and enough graham crackers, marshmallows, and chocolate bars to make s'mores for the entire Gilead Conference Center.

After returning to the beach house and making several trips up and down the lane to shuttle in the groceries, she settled into an overstuffed chair facing the deck, with a lapful of photo albums she'd taken from the steamer trunk that served as a coffee table.

Selecting an album with garish orange, pink, and green satiny swirls on the cover, she flipped slowly through the pages.

Ellen, in a yellow bikini, lying on her back on a beach towel at Pere Marquette Park, waving and smiling at the camera.

A half-dozen girls at a church retreat, stacked on a bunk bed on the verge of collapse.

A picture of herself astride Doak, the horse nearest to dead at the Spoelstra farm, where she and her best friend, Lynn, had rented out horses every day of their thirteenth summer.

Slumber party scenes. Cousins' birthday parties.

Then the picture she was searching for.

Her mother, seated at the piano beside her, a Bach piece open in front of the two of them. Mona paused and ran her finger over the image. Her mother, always the ham, had not looked toward the camera that day. Instead, she had angled herself toward Mona on the bench, her right hand poised above the keyboard, her left on Mona's back. Mona could still feel the brush of her mother's arm against hers.

A random moment, a mother and daughter sitting close, frozen in time. And in the corner of the picture, Gram's rocker nestled beside a sprawling fern.

Mona coaxed the picture from the black corner mounts that held it and placed it carefully in the padded envelope she'd bought. By the time Hallie and Dan returned, it had disappeared into a side pouch in her purse.

The entire population of the conference center didn't appear after all. Instead, a few kids Mona knew from the neighborhood drifted down with Hallie and Dan and made quiet conversation around a campfire while they roasted hotdogs and inhaled s'mores. Several swam, but by nine thirty, everyone had said polite good-byes and thanked Mona for the hospitality. No one mentioned Stacy, and it was an awkward omission that hung in the air.

Mona was washing up in the kitchen when Hallie came in for the night, sunburn lighting her cheeks and nose. The shadows had disappeared from beneath her eyes, Mona noted. A small thing, but wasn't God in the small things?

They were settled in bed, Mona in her room and Hallie in the loft, when Hallie called out the answer to the question that Mona had forgotten to ask.

"We won."

Two words. But Mona held them close as she prayed herself to sleep.

Chapter Twelve

The phone rang at seven thirty the next morning as Mona was enjoying a glass of orange juice on the deck. She knew it would be Ellen. She was predictable, if nothing else. She'd called each morning while her daughter was still asleep, always asking Mona to wake her. Her sister knew full well that Hallie had a long list of dislikes, and topping that list was waking up in the morning on anything other than her own timeline.

So it was no surprise to Mona that the daily phone conversations hadn't gone particularly well—Ellen pressing for emotional disclosure and Hallie evading with superficialities. Hallie asking to go back to bed and Ellen lashing out in a childish verbal barrage. They had honed the dance over years of practice. And today they would practice again, Mona told herself as she dug the cell phone out of the pocket of her robe.

"Hello, Mona. Can I speak to Hallie?"

"Of course. You want me to wake her?"

"Of course."

Mona sighed, then walked back into the house as she spoke. "We're planning on heading to Stewartville today so I can catch up on a little business." She tucked the phone between her shoulder and her chin, gripping her robe in one hand as she climbed the ladder to the loft. When her eyes came level with the floor, she scanned the room. A pile of blankets lay folded neatly under the window, a Tweety Bird pillow tossed to the side.

Hallie was gone.

For a moment, Mona thought she might lose her grip on the rungs and plunge to the living-room floor. Later, she wouldn't remember how she got back down. But she would remember the half-lie wrapped around a kernel of hope that she spoke to her sister.

"She's in the bathroom getting ready, Ellen. I'll have her call you back."

Hallie was not in the bathroom. Or the guestroom. Or on the porch. Mona's heart raced as she tore open a kitchen drawer and searched for the phone book and Dan's number. It rang seven agonizing times before the answering machine picked up.

Mona's eyes scanned the counters for a note but found nothing. She grabbed a key from a dish on the counter, threw open the back door, and raced down the lane, her heart pounding. The box truck was parked under a giant oak where she'd left it. She ran to the shed and turned the key in the padlock, flinging open one of the heavy wooden doors. The Fat Boy rested on its kickstand in the middle of the shed, draped in a sheet.

Only the beach was left, stretching out for miles. Or the lake . . . but she didn't want to think about the lake.

She knew Ellen would be calling back any minute. There was really only one choice. She ran back up the lane to the house and onto the porch, tossing the phone into her chair on the deck. Then she headed down the beach toward Gilead.

Hallie was surprised to be awakened by the first fingers of light peeking through the high window near the eaves. The digital alarm clock read 6:07 AM. It took her only a moment to decide. She tossed back the covers and quietly slipped into her shorts and a top. She'd waited long enough. Aunt Mona wouldn't be awake for another hour. She slid noiselessly down the ladder to the living room and headed toward the beach.

Mona was barely twenty yards from the house when she rounded a hillock and tripped on something in the sand. She thudded to the ground, sprawling unceremoniously in a heap near the remains of the evening's makeshift fire pit, scooping a cloud of sand into her mouth as she fell. For a moment, she lay choking and spitting as she struggled for breath.

"In a bit of a hurry, don't you think?"

Still spewing sand, Mona rolled onto her back just inches from Hallie, who was lying stretched out on her back, her eyes half closed. She sat up and brushed the spray of sand from her legs.

"And I believe an 'excuse me' might be in order. You nearly broke my leg." She shook the sand from her shirt.

Mona counted to five, then decided on ten as she gingerly tested her arms and legs and wiped the sand from her eyes.

"I am trying to think of one good reason why I shouldn't strangle you right now, Hallie Bowen, and I can't come up with a single one. But a woman my age shouldn't have to come face-to-face with a bail bondsman for the first time, especially without having her makeup or hair done, so you'd better start talking if you value your life."

Hallie wrinkled her nose. "I'm a little confused, mainly due to the fact I was just lying here minding my own business and you came stampeding out of nowhere and practically trampled me, accusing me that something is *my* fault. Seems to me that an apology is in order on *your* part, but hey, I'm known to be the forgiving type.

"And not to change the subject, but did you

know that Dan comes down to the beach early in the morning and brings Lum breakfast? I saw them together the other day, so this morning I decided to sit in the sword grass and watch. It's kind of cool, don't you think, to just *do* that for somebody? Just help them out for no reason?"

Mona wiped the sand from her forehead and sighed. She allowed herself another moment to consider the strangling option, then decided against it.

"Hallie, do you have any idea what I've been doing for the past ten minutes?"

"Not a clue."

"Well, I woke up to discover you were gone, so I've been tearing around the cabin and down the lane looking for you. You scared me half out of my skull!"

Hallie cocked her head and looked directly into Mona's eyes. "And why exactly were you scared?"

Mona didn't answer. Her mind raced for the right words, but they wouldn't come.

"Why were you scared, Aunt Mona? Was it because you thought I'd run away again? Or was it because you thought I'd done something to hurt myself?" Her tone was sharp.

"Hallie, I wasn't sure what you might do. I just reacted. I had to find you. Your mother called and was asking for you, and I didn't know what to say. I could hardly tell her that I didn't know where you were. What kind of reaction do you think that would have gotten? We would have had the Coast Guard and a SWAT team here in ten minutes."

"But in the middle of all of that, you wondered if I'd gone off somewhere to hurt myself." It was a statement and not a question.

"And would you?"

Hallie wrapped her arms around her legs and rested her chin on her knees. "I'm not sure."

"Then it's all right if I wasn't sure either?"

There was no answer. Finally, Hallie spoke.

"I want you to tell me something."

"Are you changing the subject?"

"Yes."

"Why?"

"Because it's something I need to know, and I was thinking about it this morning when I came down to the beach. If you answer this question for me, I'll answer your question."

"Seems fair."

"So if you wear Gram's ring all the time, how come you never wear Grandpa's? I know you have it—Mom told me."

Mona looked down to brush the sand from her arms and closed her eyes.

"You gotta tell me the real truth, Aunt Mona. I've got to be able to trust you for that."

They were both silent for a very long time, and then the words poured out of Mona like a boil that had been lanced.

"The real truth? I guess that would be because I've struggled with being mad at Grandpa for a long time. Mad because he never loved your mother or me or your grandma the way I thought he should. I think he tried, but I just never felt it.

"He did some good things. He always provided everything we needed, but I wanted his approval. I wanted him to really see into the heart of me. I always wondered if he ever really saw my mom that way."

Mona paused and fingered the ring for a moment.

"I think I always loved the breakwater at Pere Marquette Park because it's the one place I saw my dad really look at my mom, really see her. Your mom and I must have been about eight and ten. It was a Sunday afternoon, and we'd gone out for a walk to the lighthouse after church. I remember turning around and seeing them holding hands and looking at each other, and thinking for the first time that my parents really loved each other. I don't remember ever seeing that again."

Mona paused as she swallowed.

"And I'm mad because, when Gram was dying of cancer, he made it seem unspiritual to grieve about it, to talk about it. When she died, I never saw him cry. Not once, and I decided that meant he didn't care. That made it easier for me to be mad at him. And then he sold her stuff, and it just felt like there was nothing left of her. So I made it his fault because I wanted it to be his fault. I decided I didn't want to wear his ring because I didn't want to remember how he'd hurt me. Pretty messed up for a grown-up, don't you think?"

Mona felt the tears on her cheeks, but she didn't move to brush them away. Hallie scrunched a few inches closer to her in the sand, staring out toward the open water.

"I knew most of it. Not all of it, but that you were mad at him. Mom's mad, too." Hallie swept the sand on both sides of her back and forth beneath her palm.

"So why did you ask?" Mona's curiosity was genuine.

"Sometimes you just need to hear yourself say things out loud, don't you think?"

Mona smiled at the simple truth. "Yes, I do. And what do you need to hear yourself saying out loud?"

Hallie's hands stilled, and she leaned back on her elbows in the sand and stared at the sky. "I need to hear myself say that I won't hurt myself, even if I'm not sure I believe it. And I need to talk about the nightmare. Not now, but I need to tell you about all of it, soon. And then you can decide if I'm worth forgiving, too."

At that moment, Mona recognized the power of woundedness. Of Hallie's, and of her own.

Ellen had been irate, and rightfully so, Mona told her. The hardest part was admitting to the lie.

"The truth is, Ellen, at the moment you called, I didn't know exactly where Hallie was and I didn't want to scare you. So I made the excuse about the bathroom, which wasn't exactly true—no, which wasn't true at all—and I went looking for her. It wasn't right of me, and I'm sorry. I left my phone on the deck and found her on the beach, and I couldn't hear you trying to call me back."

The yelling had lasted a full ten minutes, and then Hallie had taken the phone and forced the sweetness into her voice that her mother was desperate to hear. Mona listened from her bedroom as Hallie spun soothing pleasantries about the volleyball tournament and the friends she'd met at Gilead. Mona envisioned the strain ebbing from her sister's voice. They hung up with Hallie's promise to call the next morning when they arrived in Stewartville. Mona set the alarm on her cell phone for seven o'clock to remind them.

But it was not the conversation with Ellen that Mona felt hung in the air as she and Hallie packed up the few things they would need for two days away. The words spoken on the beach had just been a beginning, and Mona and Hallie both knew it.

They were turning onto I-96 near Fruitport when Elsie called. Hallie's feet were propped on the dashboard, a steno pad on her knees as Mona dictated a list of things to do when they got to the shop. The minute Mona saw the number on the caller ID, she knew she was most likely in trouble.

"Nearly ten thirty, so I s'pose you're on the road?"

"Yes, Elsie," Mona yelled over the sound of the engine and the wind as she drummed her fingers on the steering wheel.

"Get a decent breakfast in you and that child?"

Mona looked at the candy bar she'd dropped into her lap to answer the telephone. It was one of those moments when she knew it would be better to put something in her mouth than to regret something that might come out of it. She made a quick grab for the candy and chomped off a rather large bite.

"Hallie's eating granola and strawberries right now." Mona gestured at the bag on the seat, and Hallie dutifully selected a few strawberries and a trail mix granola bar.

"Good morning, Mrs. McFeeney," Hallie called out over the roar of the engine as she ripped open the package.

"Tell the child good morning for me," Elsie commanded, and Mona obeyed.

"Shouldn't be talking on the phone while you're driving, so I need to make this short."

Mona controlled the urge to say that the only reason she was talking on the phone while she was driving was because Elsie had called her in the first place.

"I just wanted you to know there's a head-turnin' surprise for you when you get here, unless it's somethin' you already know about. I don't s'pose you already know about it, do you?"

"About what?" Mona's voice was edged with exasperation, and with Elsie, exasperation always seemed to come hand-in-hand with guilt. Mona had never quite figured out why, and she wasn't sure she ever would.

" 'Bout the delivery."

Mona took a bite of a huge strawberry. "Well, of course I know about the delivery. It's a piecrust table from Elmer Dean's."

"Sure as I'm standin' here, that would be a no. This here's no piecrust table."

"Well then what *is* it, Elsie?" Mona moaned. A bag of M&M's suddenly seemed to be calling her name. She calculated how far it was to the next gas station. Ten miles, max.

"I'm guessin' it's a surprise, so I'm not gonna tell you. Somebody rang the delivery bell this morning at eight dad-blame o'clock before we'd opened, but by the time I got to the back room, they'd drove off. I barely got a look at the truck.

But there's a letter with it, so I s'pose you'll know the answer soon enough. Just thought you needed to know."

"To know what?"

But Elsie was already gone.

"What was that all about?" Hallie asked.

"You've got me. Elsie says I have some kind of a present waiting for me at the shop, and she won't give me a clue what it is."

"Cool," Hallie said as she stuck another strawberry in her mouth. "What do you hope it is?"

"Maybe a red Porsche. Or a pain-free, noninvasive home liposuction machine. What about you?"

Hallie rested her head against the rear window of the truck and thought a moment.

"A necklace."

Mona glanced at her niece. "A necklace? You hardly ever wear jewelry, even the diamond stud earrings I had made for you from Gram's jewelry when you got your ears pierced a few years ago. I can't remember ever seeing you wear a necklace."

Hallie closed her eyes. "Well I have." Her eyes were closed tightly.

She turned her face toward the window, and Mona knew the conversation was over. And she knew that it was something Hallie had had to say out loud, for whatever reason. But before they reached the village limits of Stewartville, an image slowly took shape in her mind, a scene coming in and out of focus in waves of memory.

Two girls playing at the water's edge, one wearing a heart-shaped necklace, the other yelling something Mona couldn't quite remember.

And then the part of the scene she couldn't forget. Herself turning and walking away for the five minutes that changed everything.

Chapter Thirteen

They pulled into Stewartville at one o'clock, after a stop at the Greenville Meijer store to pick up a few extra clothes for Hallie. Mona knew that Ellen would be horrified that she'd bought her daughter a pair of jeans and two tops for less than thirty dollars in a store where toilet plungers were displayed just yards away from women's lingerie. But utility had always been more important than fashion in Mona's mind, and the child needed clothes for the few days of hauling files and cleaning the office that Mona had planned. She could only imagine Ellen's anger if Hallie returned home with stains on her hundred-dollar blue jeans.

Mona pulled down the alley into her spot behind the shop and threw the truck into park. Grabbing her purse, she scrambled out the door and headed toward the back entry. Hallie's door slammed behind her.

"A little anxious to unpack that liposuction machine, don't you think?"

Mona laughed and stopped in the middle of the alley.

"Hurry up, girl, and yes, I am. It's not every day an unmarried woman who grew up thinking the Lone Ranger was a stud gets surprise mystery gifts. I just hope it's worth breaking the speed limit for, because I'm pretty sure Officer Spencer just got a shot of me with his new radar gun. Front page news for the *Sentinel* a few weeks ago, that new gun, blast it."

The back door of the shop burst open, and Mona turned to find Elsie blocking the doorway, her hands on her hips. She was wearing a plaid periwinkle cobbler apron over a yellow blouse and yellow slacks, and her miniscule sneakers were a perfectly matching blue. Everyone in Stewartville knew that Elsie dyed her shoes herself, a veritable shoe rainbow that punctuated other equally alarming ensembles.

It took Mona a moment to realize that Hallie was staring, but Elsie didn't seem to notice.

"Get over here, girl, and let me get a look at you. Don't go standin' there just takin' up space. I am a hugger—everyone knows it—so just get over here."

Mona watched uncertainly as Hallie hesitated, then walked toward Elsie, encircled her tiny frame in her tanned arms, and lifted her from her feet in a huge bear hug. She giggled as she swung the tiny woman in a slow circle. It was the giggle of a child, a giggle Mona hadn't heard in a long time.

"How's that, Mrs. McFeeney?"

Elsie struggled for her balance for a moment as Hallie planted her back on her feet. Then she threw her head back and laughed.

"That's just fine, Miss Hallie Bowen. Just fine." She turned toward Mona. "And you, Miss Mona, look like you could use an iced tea. There's Coke in the fridge for Hallie, and I brought potato salad and sandwiches from home. I can't imagine the kind of whatnot you probably been feedin' that girl these past three days. Now get in here. Hallie, you can haul the food to the table in the front room."

She waved them on into the shop, then scurried to a dented refrigerator in a corner of the back room, threw open the door, and began rummaging inside.

"Where's Harold?" Mona asked, plopping her purse onto a walnut gateleg table near the back-room door and glancing around the shop. She watched as Hallie dutifully followed Elsie to the fridge and stood with outstretched arms as she was piled high with Tupperware.

"Sent him to my house to check on the dogs and rest a spell in my hammock. Needed a nap, that one. And just where do you think you're goin', missy?"

Mona had moved toward the door that separated the back room from the front of the shop.

"Gotta wait," Elsie said flatly as she banged the refrigerator door closed with a hip. "No snoopin'."

"And I'd like to know why," Mona challenged as she stepped through the open doorway into the shop showroom, wondering for a moment if she'd be sent to a corner for a timeout. "If I'm not mistaken, I'm the boss around here," she called over her shoulder.

"Well that for sure ain't the first time you been mistaken. And anybody who knows you knows it sure won't be the last. We're havin' a nice lunch together first so's I can have some plain talk with this child who's responsible for the calluses on my knees. And if you're lookin' for that box, you don't know where it is, and I'm not about to tell you until I get some answers from Miss Hallie here. Now set yourself down while I get this lunch spread out on the table."

Mona opened her mouth, but words wouldn't come. She stared silently as Elsie herded Hallie toward a mammoth trestle table, unloaded her arms, and heaped paper plates with potato salad and apple crisp, hemmed in by golden croissants stacked with ham and cheese.

Mona knew she was beaten. She couldn't remember the last time an argument with Elsie had been worth the effort. She chose a facade of silent grace and took her place on the bench seat across from Hallie while Elsie returned to the back room and came back carrying tall glasses of iced tea. She planted them firmly in the middle of the table, wiped her hands on her cobbler apron, and tilted her head back as if she'd spotted something remarkable on the pressed-tin ceiling.

"Lord God, forgive us for not having the good sense to be thankful for who You are and what You've done for us. Thank You for not giving up on us when we deserve it. Thank You for seeing who You want us to be instead of who we mostly tend to be. Amen."

Mona saw the old woman's lips move almost imperceptibly for a moment before she lowered her eyes slowly, drawing Hallie into her gaze.

"So, Miss Hallie, I've been on my knees nearly every hour since your aunt lit out of here lookin' for you. What do you have to say for yourself?"

Mona watched silently as Hallie's eyes widened, flickering in uncertainty as she glanced toward her aunt.

Mona shrugged. "You're on your own, girl."

A periwinkle foot began to tap, and Mona smiled. This was going to get interesting. Hallie's eyes flickered back to Elsie.

"I . . . I guess I should say . . . what I mean is . . . okay, I'll just say it. Thank you. For the prayers, I mean."

Mona made an effort to keep her mouth from falling open.

The tapping stopped.

"So that's somethin' you think is important, then, people's prayers?"

Hallie's gaze remained fixed on Elsie's face.

"Sometimes. I was praying as we drove into Stewartville that Aunt Mona wouldn't get a speeding ticket for going sixty in a thirty-five. And when she took us out on my dad's Harley the other night, I prayed that she'd remember how to clutch and shift at the same time. And since that's more than any prayers I've said for the past two years, it's a pretty big start for me. So I guess I do . . . think it's important . . . I guess."

She exhaled loudly and her shoulders slumped a bit, as if someone had just let the air out of her. Elsie cleared her throat and seemed for the moment to be at a loss for words. Hallie squirmed slightly. Mona brushed imaginary lint from her jeans and stood.

"I have two announcements to make. The first is that having Hallie here with me at this moment is an answer to my deepest prayers. Thank you, Elsie, for your prayers on Hallie's behalf. I cannot thank you enough, my friend."

She reached across the table for Elsie's hand, raised it to her face, and brushed it with a kiss.

"Well, then."

The old woman's face was obscured through the blur of Mona's tears.

"And the second announcement is that I am

going to pretend that I'm actually in charge of this shop, even though everyone present knows I'm really not. And I have decided that it's time to see what's behind Door Number One. Please, Elsie."

She smiled sweetly, like a pleading child.

Elsie scowled, then pulled an envelope from her cobbler apron and placed it in Mona's hand.

"This came with it. Maybe you should read it first. Been drivin' me crazy, not knowin' what's in there."

Mona tore open the envelope and read the words silently. A single sentence in block letters, bearing the watery black strokes of a fountain pen.

"Well?" Hallie asked.

Mona shook her head and read the words slowly.
A treasure from the past to cherish for tomorrow. Blessings.

"It's the slogan for the shop. It doesn't make any sense."

"I think it does," Elsie said as she beckoned the two of them to follow her up the stairs to the loft. Mona raced up the dozen steps. Hallie scrambled behind her, and the two waited on the landing outside the closed door of Mona's apartment as Elsie followed behind at a slightly more deliberate pace. When she reached the landing, she gave Mona a nod. Mona pushed open the heavy oak door and gasped.

A spindle-armed rocker stood in the center of the floor of the spacious studio apartment, like a car in a showroom. She drew in a long breath as she walked slowly across the room, not believing what she saw.

"This can't be it. It can't be! Hallie, come here. Look, the initials, *H* and *S*." She ran her hands along the arms. "And the teeth marks in the arms and the gouges on the back." Her eyes traced every detail. "I can't believe it. It's hers. It's Mom's."

She turned and lowered herself into the seat.

"Who found it? Elsie, it was you, wasn't it?"

Elsie shook her head, and a lavender tendril wafted near her neck.

"No sirree, Bob. I had nothin' to do with this. Must have been someone you called while you were down there in Muskegon."

Mona searched her memory. She had to have called at least ten dealers to ask about the chair.

"But who would just give it to me and not tell me who they are? Why would they do that?"

Elsie turned toward the door.

"Durned if I know, but I guess it's your job to think on that. I'm gonna head back down with Hallie, and we're gonna get a start on our lunch. You just take a little time." She took Hallie gently by the arm, and the door closed behind them.

Mona eased into the chair and ran her fingers up and down the arms as she leaned back. She closed her eyes until the pictures came.

Pictures of her mother sitting in the chair knitting—blankets for friends, lap throws for shut-ins, baby blankets for young mothers.

And a red afghan.

Or snapping beans and peeling potatoes into a dutch oven in the years when the cancer had weakened her and the chair had been brought into the kitchen. Then another image took shape.

A young wife blurring into middle age as she grew gaunt and pale with disease.

A wife who had prayed over an open Bible for a husband whose faith had been visible only as the dimmest of shadows.

Mona's thoughts drifted to her father, and for the first time in many months, she let them come. Stark memories of the man who measured all things against himself—his intellect, his finances, his accomplishments. She had been just a child when the realization had taken root in her heart that he had measured her in all things as well, and she had always been found wanting.

Mona rubbed her hands on the rounded curve of the arm. This had been the chair he had always chosen for their Sunday game of chess. A game of logic with no room for error or chance. He had never played with her mother or Ellen, and Mona had never known why. For years she had sat in the shadow he cast across the table, watching him place his pieces in the center of the squares with obsessive precision. And on the rare occasion that he lost a pawn or a rook to her strategy, the vanquished were lined up at the right side of the board in straight rows of four, edges touching.

How this man had come to marry a woman as joyous and radiant as her mother was a mystery Mona had never fathomed. When they were teenagers, she and Ellen had even spun conspiratorial theories. But to have asked her mother would have been a betrayal, and as they grew older, the question had been abandoned.

Hallie's question drifted in and out of her thoughts as she slowly rocked.

Why don't you wear Grandpa's ring?

She knew that before she rose from the chair she had to face the answer, had to say the words out loud, if only to herself.

The sound of laughter drifted up from the shop. Hallie knew. Hallie had said it.

Some things aren't worth forgiving.

It was a lie they shared, and Mona was sick with the realization.

An hour later, when Mona descended the stairs dressed in crisp khaki shorts and a chambray short-sleeved shirt, she found the polished pine trestle table had been cleared and wiped clean. It didn't surprise her. For Elsie, there was a time and place for everything. A time for thinking, a time for eating. And always, a time for speaking her mind.

Mona headed toward the back room and the

refrigerator, where she knew she'd find a neatly wrapped plate intended to save her from death by mayonnaise. Elsie was Stewartville's watchdog on the dangers of food left out longer than it took to chew it and swallow it. She was also known to wax eloquent on the hazards of raw cookie dough, which was one of Mona's favorite food groups, right next to chocolate. In Elsie's opinion, Mona daily flouted death by eating her own cooking.

She passed the office door and caught a glimpse of Elsie's cotton-candy hair peeking over a pile of files stacked on the massive cherry desk that had commanded her father's study for as long as she could remember. To the side of the desk, near a wall of filing cabinets, Hallie leaned back at a perilous angle in a scarred leather office chair, wadding papers one-by-one from a stack in her lap and lobbing them toward a half-full metal trash can near the door.

"Feel like a walk, Hal?" Mona called over her shoulder as she opened the refrigerator door and stuck her head inside. She grabbed the plate she found on the top shelf and slid aside a pile of Tupperware on the shelf below to claim a can of Diet Coke.

"Where?"

Mona walked back into the front room and stepped into the office, leaning against the wall near the door. "To get Oscar, with maybe a few errands thrown in."

Hallie slowly wadded another paper and took aim.

"I'm just kinda getting into my groove here. I'm fifteen for seventeen."

Elsie's voice came from behind the stack of files.

"And in about five minutes, she's runnin' up to your bedroom closet and draggin' down a few more boxes for me to sort through so's I can rest easy that the IRS isn't comin' to drag us all away."

Mona set the plate on a bookshelf and grabbed the sandwich as she turned toward the door.

"Then I'm getting out of here while the gettin's good. I'll bring you two a pint of Moose Tracks from the Dairy Delight. I'll be back before supper." She was out the door before Elsie had a chance to respond.

The summer heat hit her like a slap as she headed up Main Street, but it felt good, good to be home, where by now everyone knew she had returned with her wayward niece, even though she hadn't spoken to a single soul since they'd pulled into town. It was one thing she'd quickly learned about Stewartville. People knew what you'd eaten for breakfast before you had a chance to get hungry for lunch. Officer Spencer would have radioed Nellie Krell back at city hall the minute he'd seen Mona shoot past his speed trap. And Nellie would have told everyone who stopped by to shoot the breeze or catch up on village politics.

Within minutes, words would have hit Trina's Café and the crowd at the Curl Up and Dye. Even as she walked down the street, Mona knew she was a marked woman. Everyone would be looking for her, and everyone would be asking. But for now, she had nothing to say. Hallie was all right, and Hallie was with her. A prayer of thanks rose in her heart as she hurried her footsteps.

It was a quick walk, just two blocks to the police station and city hall. Mona was glad she'd taken time to fill out the check for one hundred dollars from the shrinking inheritance fund before she'd come down the stairs from the apartment. She made the visit short and sweet, breezing in and out so fast that Nellie didn't have time to spit out a single question.

"Sorry, Nellie, I've got to run. The note explains it all," she'd called back as the door swung shut behind her. Mona laughed to herself as she caught a glimpse of a bewildered Nellie with check in hand, staring at the cryptic memo Mona had scrawled on a sticky note in sweeping flourishes:

Sorry, Officer Spencer. I figured sixty in a thirty-five would be about a hundred bucks. I didn't deserve the break. If no ticket was issued, please ask Nellie to apply the funds to the playground renovation in the city park, in memory of William and Jean VanderMolen.

It was one of the things Mona knew she had to put right before the day ended. The other would take longer.

She dug into the pocket of her jeans and ran her fingers across the worn leather of a small white New Testament as she turned left and headed up Maple Street toward the park. She prayed she would find solitude there.

It would be almost dinnertime before she returned home with a crazed Oscar and a quiet heart. And Hallie didn't seem to notice that Mona had forgotten the Moose Tracks. Once again, she seemed lost in her own world, and Mona let her be. She knew the look of guilt in her niece's eyes. It had been there too long for her not to recognize it.

When Hallie asked to go home with Elsie for the night, Mona quietly said yes, no questions asked. Just the questions in her heart. How could she reach a child who had turned to stone, and in just a few short days?

It was a truth Mona had known in the core of her being from the moment she had seen Hallie on the beach-house deck. She couldn't change her. She was helpless to change anything in Hallie's heart that Hallie didn't first want to change herself.

It was a truth that drove Mona to her knees far into the night.

Chapter Fourteen

At 6:05, Mona awoke to a familiar flapping of ears and a gentle whining. She'd come to depend on the fact that Oscar's bladder was more reliable than any alarm clock, although she'd never had to walk her alarm clock the daunting distance to the alley in the early morning hours. She reluctantly threw back the covers and lifted the densely packed dog to the floor.

A glass of orange juice and a bagel later, Mona stood at the door of the office in her favorite yellow muslin nightgown, surveying the room and its ominous stacks of files as Oscar luxuriated in a heap of fleecy blankets on her bedroom floor. She didn't know whether to feel sick or grateful. Elsie had obviously jumped into the task of sorting files with the tenacity of a pit bull. Twenty years of yellowed receipt books filled four plastic milk crates stacked to the right of the door, and a dozen or so dusty file boxes surrounded the enormous desk like football players in a huddle, waiting for the next call. Hallie's shooting percentage had apparently paid off. The trash can was mounded in a heap of crisp snowballs nearly waist high. An avalanche had apparently occurred during the night, and a pile of books stacked along the right-hand wall beneath an aerial print of Stewartville had slid into the center of the room in an artistic swath.

Mona heaved a sigh and stepped into the room, carefully gathering the length of her nightgown and hoisting it to knee-level as she navigated her way to the desk through a narrow path of boxes, crates, and office equipment. It was worse than she'd expected, but then, why wouldn't it be? The people side of the business had been her strength from the beginning, and the details of book-keeping, taxes, and inventories had pulled at her like the weight of an anchor.

If Ellen could see me now, she'd laugh, Mona thought as she dropped into the leather chair, taking in the disarray around her. A Stewartville centennial blanket lay in a heap at her feet, and the contents of a half-eaten bag of pork rinds lay scattered across the top of the copy machine. Hallie's contribution to the office decor. Her eyes fell on the accounting ledger in the center of the desk, the letter from Eskel Barkel peeking out from the top, bookmarking a page with too much inventory and too few sales.

The thought echoed through her mind as she stared at the black book. *Maybe they were right after all.* Her friends, Ellen, everyone who'd told her she was crazy to think she could make a success of an obscure antique shop in an even more obscure town. Mona pulled the letter from between the pages of the ledger and clasped it between her palms as she spoke into the room.

"Lord, I don't know if I can do this. All of this—

Hallie, the shop. You've got to direct my feet for the next step. Some days I feel like it might be time to go back to teaching. I don't have to keep this place; I can give it up if that's what You want. But I can't give up on Hallie, because I know You haven't given up on her." She paused for a moment. "And I know You haven't given up on me. I know You're asking me to lay it all down, to do the hard work in my own heart so I can show Hallie how to do it in hers. I know I'm not done with forgiving my dad, that I'm still blaming him. I know my hardest work doesn't have anything to do with this shop."

Her lips continued to move as the moments slipped away. Then, like a schoolchild, she laid her head on her arms and rested.

The front door slammed with the sound of a gunshot. Mona was jolted awake. Staccato footsteps on the squeaky hardwood floor told her that Elsie and Hallie had arrived. She glanced at the wall clock near the office door and moaned. Eight thirty. Elsie would never let her live this down.

"Aunt Mona!" The sound of footsteps pounding up the stairs reverberated through the office. "I brought Elsie's warm cinnamon rolls with extra frosting. She stopped at Trina's to get some coffee and have a chat. Where are you?" A door creaked open above, then slammed shut again.

"In the office, Hal," Mona called as she ran her

fingers quickly through her hair and slipped the letter back into the ledger.

A second door slammed, this time from the rear of the shop as the sound of Hallie's footsteps pounded back down the stairs. Mona glanced up as a body appeared in the office doorway, but it wasn't Hallie. A tall man wearing a pale green polo shirt and jeans stared back at her through sunglass-shaded eyes.

"Excuse me for just walking in. The alley door was marked 'Deliveries,' and your sign says you open at eight thirty. No one answered when I knocked, so I thought I'd check and see if someone was here."

The man paused for Mona's response, but no words came except for the silent prayer that she was the only person aware that she was sitting at the desk in her nightgown. She reached slowly for the blanket on the floor as she struggled to maintain what she hoped was a professional expression.

"Aunt Mona?" The voice came from behind the broad shoulders, and the man stepped quickly to the side, revealing a rather puzzled Hallie staring into the office. Mona took advantage of the split second to throw the blanket over her shoulders and gather it tightly around her.

"Right here, Hal. I'm afraid you've both caught me a bit off guard. I came down early this morning with Oscar, and I'm afraid I fell asleep here at the desk." She ran her fingers through her hair once again and cast a bleak smile in the direction of the doorway.

The man glanced at the paper he held in his hand, then looked back toward Mona, smiling.

"I assume, then, that you're Mona VanderMolen, the owner?"

He slid his sunglasses to the top of his head, revealing deep brown eyes.

Mona noted the sunglasses and close-cropped sandy hair. Something stirred in her memory. And there was something in the voice. She searched his face and guessed him to be forty-five or fifty, but she couldn't place him.

"No. I mean, yes. I am Mona VanderMolen, and I'm the owner."

The man smiled and pointed to Hallie, who was watching the interaction with a growing smile on her face.

"So this isn't your daughter? Amazing. From a distance, you could pass for twins." He crossed his tan arms. The pale green of his short-sleeved polo showed off his deep tan.

Hallie laughed. "Now there's an original come-on, but how about I give you a hand here? She's single, no kids, no boyfriend. And a terrific cook."

"Hallie!" Mona's voice cut through the room, and her face flushed. For a moment she felt like she was in the junior high lunchroom again and Beverly Wilson was hollering to the whole room that Mona VanderMolen had never been kissed and any guy who'd like to help her out could meet her behind the band room after school.

She swallowed and softened her voice.

"I apologize for my niece's rudeness, something I have to do far too often these days. Unfortunately, she's not only rude. She's a liar. I'm a lousy cook." She drew the blanket closer. "You must be here with the piecrust table from Elmer Dean. I apologize for the totally unprofessional manner in which you were greeted here, Mr. . . ."

"Adam Dean."

"Mr. Dean."

"Adam."

"Adam, then." Mona smiled politely and stepped gingerly around the desk, clutching the blanket around her. "I don't suppose you have a pen handy to sign for the delivery? I'm not sure I can find one in this mess right now. We're undergoing renovation, as you can see. And I would be personally grateful if Hallie could sign for me."

Once again she blushed and tightened her grip on the blanket. *A whack job,* she told herself. *The man must think I'm positively nuts.* She glared at Hallie and wondered if the temporary-insanity plea had a special application for parents of teenagers.

Adam pulled a pen from his back pocket and handed it to Hallie, whose smile spread from ear to ear as she scrawled her signature and handed back the pen with a dramatic flourish. Mona thought for a moment about crawling under her desk to hide as she forced her most professional tone.

"If you would be so kind as to bring the table to the front of the shop for me, Adam. I'd like it to have the greatest possible exposure right in front. The workmanship is extraordinary, and I only wish I had a few more of the craftsman's pieces to display."

Adam smiled, an easy smile that spread across his face until it reached his eyes. Mona noticed the deep crinkles that extended from the corners and deepened with the warm grin. Laugh wrinkles. She had always approved of laugh wrinkles, especially her own. She found herself smiling back.

"I actually have a few additional pieces in the back of my Suburban, if you'd like to take the time to see them. I'm taking them to a conference center today as part of a presentation. I've been asked to provide furnishings for some of the common areas in their lodge."

"Really?" Mona was surprised at the intensity of the single word, and she felt the color rise in her face again. Was it her imagination, or had her voice sounded about twenty decibels too loud? But Adam didn't seem to notice. He uncrossed his arms.

"I've got a few extra minutes before I have to

get on the road. I could take you out back and show you some of the pieces if you have time." He pointed to the trestle table. "I could have a seat and take one of those cinnamon rolls off your hands while you get ready. Unless, of course, this small town is different from the one I live in, where news of a strange man and a single woman in a nightgown standing together in an alley in the morning would provide grist for the gossip mill for about ten years. I don't mean to sound forward. I just thought you might feel more comfortable if I gave you an opportunity to gracefully escape."

Mona's face glowed fire hot as she searched for a proper reply, but none came, and her eyes flickered to the floor as a wave of self-consciousness washed over her.

"I'll be glad to get you a paper plate for that cinnamon roll, Mr. Dean, while my Aunt Mona changes," Hallie offered quickly. "I'm sure she'd like to check out what you have. Now hurry along, Auntie, while I keep Mr. Dean occupied."

Mona wanted to smack the child, but she didn't trust herself to glance in Hallie's direction. She fled the room in horror, the blanket billowing around her, her bare feet slapping on the stairway as she sought temporary refuge in her bedroom. Her mind raced as she prepared mental notes for the lecture Hallie would receive the moment Adam Dean left. Five minutes later, dressed in white linen capris and a soft pink cotton blouse, she was standing in the back alley next to a dark blue Suburban as Adam licked the last vestiges of frosting from his fingers. Hallie stood behind them in the shop doorway watching. Although Mona couldn't see her, she was certain that a smirk was painted across her niece's face.

"My turn to apologize for my rudeness," Adam said as he wiped his hands on each other and reached into the pocket of his khakis for the keys to the vehicle. The sunglasses were back in place, hiding the expression in his eyes, and Mona's tension eased with the warmth in his voice. She had to hand it to him. Most men would have seized the opportunity to take advantage of Hallie's innuendos, but he'd barely seemed to notice them.

"That may be the best cinnamon roll I've ever eaten. While you were changing, your niece told me that a friend made them for you this morning. She could go into business and give Krispy Kreme a run for its money."

Mona smiled, a memory tugging at the corner of her thoughts. Then her eyes grew wide as images and sounds ricocheted through her brain like a pinball on steroids.

"Krispy Kreme?"

Adam smiled. "You know, the doughnuts. The glazed ones are my personal favorites—"

"The glazed ones? The ones with the gooey frosting that gets all over your fingers?"

Adam glanced up from sorting through the keys in his hand and threw her a puzzled look.

"Yes," he said slowly.

"Good heavens, do you know who you are?" Once again, Mona's words came out more forcefully than she had expected.

"Do I know who I am? You're kidding, right?" Adam had moved to the rear of the vehicle as he sorted through the keys.

Mona's hands flew to her hips.

"You're the dealer who bought the sideboard out from under my nose at the Bailey auction. For heaven's sake, do you know you don't even sweat like a normal person?"

A bemused look flickered across Adam's face.

"I hardly think we need to turn this into a conversation about what normal people do, seeing as how you greeted me this morning, a total stranger and a man, in your nightgown, and now you are standing in a public alley babbling about my lack of perspiring to your expectations."

For a moment, Mona was speechless. Then the undisguised sound of Hallie's laughter bubbled up behind her, and she felt her anger flare red hot, the anger of humiliation and embarrassment and too many sleepless nights. The anger that had raged against her father in the weeks after her mother's death when she'd felt invisible and worthless. The anger that had swallowed her heart in the weeks after Stacy's death, that she'd confessed again and again, and that bound her heart to Hallie's.

The words spewed from her like water gushing from a hydrant on a blazing summer day.

"And then you had the nerve to accuse me of obscenity on the telephone? I was eating a Krispy Kreme, and you treated me like a pervert! What gave you the right to make someone you don't even know feel like—like they're dirt? I'm not like that at all, for your information! How dare you insult me like that?"

From the doorway, Hallie's voice called out. "Jeez, Aunt Mona, if anyone from the *Sentinel* hears a word you're saying right now, you're gonna make the front page. You need to calm down just a tad, if you ask me."

Mona drew a deep breath and struggled to lower her voice. Her heart was racing, and her voice shook.

"Hallie, in the best interests of everyone present, I would suggest you turn around and go watch the shop for me while I conclude my conversation with Mr. Dean."

"Conversation? I'd hardly call—"

"Now!" She listened for the sound of movement behind her.

Mona's eyes were locked on Adam's face. The smile had disappeared, and she couldn't read his expression behind the dark glasses. Like a junior higher locked in a stare down, she glared back and refused to look away.

After what seemed like minutes, a door

slammed, and they stood in silence. The words that had poured from her were gone. Adam held her in a steady gaze, and she felt her cheeks flush. She was surprised when he spoke, his tone even and measured.

"I bought the sideboard for my uncle Elmer to give to my aunt for a birthday gift. He'd been looking for one like it for her for over a year, and I knew how much it would mean to both of them. I'm sorry you were the person I was bidding against. My actions at the time were certainly not personal, and I'm a bit confused as to why you would consider them so."

Mona tried to swallow, but a lump had risen in her throat. She'd acted like a fool, and she knew it. She only knew that if she spoke another word, tears would pour from her like an uncapped hydrant, and it would only get worse.

"And in regard to obscenities on the telephone, I believe that I can safely assume you are the woman who placed a call to my uncle's shop several days ago and made bizarre noises in my ear. I thought you were a fifteen-year-old kid entertaining yourself by making crank calls. I did not intend to insult you. Again, my apologies for my rudeness. Frankly, it amazes me that I've managed to offend you so many times when I've known you for less than ten minutes."

Mona took a breath to speak, but he raised his hand to silence her.

"And in regard to my sweating or lack thereof, my first response would be to tell you that you are either mentally imbalanced or amazingly impolite. But I am choosing, instead, to believe that you simply have spent too much time in the sun the past few days and that it has skewed your judgment."

He fingered the keys in his hand as he stepped back toward the driver's door of the Suburban, shaking his head.

"I placed the piecrust table in your display room while you were upstairs and left a brochure with your niece, Miss VanderMolen. It shows other historical reproductions that are available through my company. I'd recommend that you call the shop to select anything you might be interested in. My uncle will be most happy to help you. But right now, I have to get on the road. My appointment in Muskegon is at eleven."

He opened the door and slid into the driver's seat.

"I apparently didn't catch you at your best today, which I truly regret, but I think we can both agree that this interchange has been a bit uncomfortable. I don't think prolonging it will improve matters much. Now I really do have to get to my next appointment and set up my display before the board members come."

He shifted the Suburban into gear and pulled away before Mona had a chance to reply. A cloud of dust rose as he drove down the alley and turned onto Elm Street.

She wasn't sure how long she stood watching the dust drift through the rays of morning light streaking through the maples that lined the alley. She wasn't even sure what had just happened. But she was sure that somewhere in the few unsettling moments she had known Adam Dean, she had made herself look like an idiot and had been so close to the verge of tears that she could taste the salt.

But it wasn't until later in the morning that Mona began to truly understand what it meant to feel like a fool. The realization came like a lightning bolt in the moment when she asked Hallie for the receipt for the piecrust table, the moment her eyes fell on the meticulously formed block letters of the table's dimensions and description. The moment she realized that Hallie's name at the bottom had been signed with a watery fountain pen.

Chapter Fifteen

Mona was amazed that for reasons known only to God above, Hallie never breathed a word of the encounter to Elsie when she breezed in from Trina's at nine sharp. Or later in the day, for that matter, as the threesome sorted paperwork, hauled trash, and reorganized files between chats with occasional customers or friends who stopped in to size up the niece who had sent Mona running. She was more than slightly suspicious that her encounter with Adam Dean might be turned into an opportunity for blackmail, but if Hallie had something up her sleeve, she wasn't tipping her hand. She had gone strangely quiet, responding to every request to tote, sort, and pitch with an unquestioning compliance that Mona hadn't seen in years. Mona was certain that Hallie's rude behavior had been intentional, and she knew she had to confront it. But she also knew she had to do business with her own heart before she could deal with Hallie's.

It was nearly twelve thirty when Elsie dropped into the leather chair and announced that they were done for the morning. That was when Mona took her first opportunity to slip into the alley and call the cell number printed on the receipt to find out if Adam Dean had secretly sent her her mother's chair.

And to apologize, if he'd let her. She'd formed the words in her mind a hundred times, refining them with each rehearsal. In the end, she'd decided on the plain, unvarnished truth. She'd let her emotions overwhelm her and had lashed out. She'd acted like a child, and there was no excuse except that the wounded child who lived in her heart still wanted to be known for who she was, not for a distorted image of what someone else believed her to be.

But there was no answer, and when the answering machine sounded, Mona quickly hung up. It was the first of a half-dozen calls she placed that afternoon, all unanswered.

Harold came in shortly after they had finished up in the office. He was a gentle giant, more than six feet tall, with a head of straw-colored, stick-straight hair that gave him an almost boyish appearance, even at the age of seventy-nine. He was dressed in his uniform of bib overalls and a plaid collared shirt buttoned clear to his Adam's apple. People in Stewartville knew that the day Harold appeared without that top button buttoned, hell would freeze over and the Democrats would take the county elections. In fact, townspeople were pretty sure that Bernard Mason over at Mason's Funeral Home had strict instructions from Harold not to lay him out unless he was buttoned up tight in his casket.

Elsie laid out the assorted deli meats and salads as Harold carefully set his homemade french silk pie in the center of the table. Rumor had it that women all over the county secretly contracted with him for pies to take to family reunions, and if anybody could keep a secret in Stewartville, it was Harold.

Mona busied herself laying out the Royal Albert china and watched with interest as Hallie was introduced and settled herself beside the quiet, hulking man at the trestle table. His workroom had intrigued her from the moment they'd arrived, and at least once, Mona had caught Hallie examining the assortment of belt sanders, Dremels, and power tools. Within minutes, she'd launched into a barrage of questions about woodworking and refinishing techniques. Mona smiled as she retrieved silverware from a sideboard and placed it at the table settings. *Who'd a thunk it?* Everyone in Stewartville knew that Harold wasn't given much to talking, much less to teenage girls. And he wasn't a man given to easy smiles, but Mona couldn't help noting that Hallie was getting more than her fair share.

It wasn't long after lunch had been cleared away that Harold's ability to cope with three females waned, and he made polite apologies and headed to the back room. Hallie was instantly on his heels, and Mona and Elsie were left alone at the trestle table just long enough for Elsie to make an announcement.

"Gotta surprise for the two of you tonight. And don't bother goin' askin' what it is, 'cause my mouth is shut tighter'n an outhouse door in January."

But any excitement Elsie had hoped to generate with her news was cut short by the ringing of Mona's cell phone. One glance at the caller ID told her what she'd feared.

"I've got to take this, Elsie," Mona called over her shoulder as she rose and slipped from the table. Taking the stairs two at a time, she disappeared into the apartment, closing the door behind her. She whispered a silent prayer as she lifted the phone to her ear.

"Hello, Ellen."

When she came down twenty minutes later, Mona had forgotten about Elsie's surprise.

Hallie spent the afternoon with Harold in the back room, soaking in his secrets of sandpaper grits and stripping solutions. Mona stayed within earshot throughout the day as she worked on the books in the office, running back and forth to the alley every half hour to redial the number on the receipt, then rapidly clicking off at the sound of the modulated female voice telling her that her party was not available.

She worked silently alongside Elsie, listening to a litany of information about Ginny Mae's new perm, Norma Eikenberry's visit to see her brother at the Mason's Home, and Clarence Dillingham's hernia surgery. For a Baptist born and raised, Clarence had sure sworn up a blue streak in the recovery room. Ruth Cavanaugh was workin' the second shift when they brought him in, and she saw it herself. If Elsie trusted anyone's gossip, it was Ruth Cavanaugh's, chairman of the Community Church Ladies' Auxiliary.

By mid-afternoon, Mona was exhausted and sat cross-legged on the office floor near a filing cabinet whose contents had been disgorged in staggering piles that encircled her. She woodenly sorted the massive stacks of paperwork, marveling at her brain's ability to multitask as she listened to Elsie's bizarre catalog of facts and observations about the Stewartville population. At the same time, she found herself outlining the salient points of her apology to Adam Dean while praying for God's direction for the best moment to tell Hallie about her mother's call. For the first time, she was glad for Elsie's gift for one-sided conversations. She sighed heavily as she dumped a pile of yellowed receipts into a waste basket.

God, I've blown it again. I know that doesn't come as any surprise to You, and I don't know why it does to me. I'm so graceless sometimes—with Hallie, with Ellen, with people I hardly even know. Forgive me. Make me a mirror of Your grace, Lord, and give me the wisdom I so desperately need to show Hallie and my sister how much You love them. And assuming that amnesia is not in Your plan for Adam Dean, allow me an opportunity to apologize to him in a way that would honor You.

For once, Mona was glad that the shop was quiet except for a few window shoppers who glimpsed the piecrust table through the beveled-glass front door and wandered in to admire it. Francie Effingham even ran over from the *Sentinel* and snapped a shot, asking Mona for the history of the actual table in the Smithsonian Institute and whether or not she would be carrying any more of the craftsman's pieces on a regular basis. In her most businesslike tone, Mona stated that she didn't know at this time but was currently investigating a variety of options for the future of her business. Eskel Barkel's letter loomed in her mind as she spoke the words, but she pushed the thought away.

At three o'clock, Elsie ran home to let Tessa out for her afternoon constitutional, and Mona headed up to the apartment to bring Oscar down for his nap in the swath of afternoon sun that fell in the display window. Elsie had announced she would be gone for at least an hour, and Mona knew she couldn't wait any longer. She had to tell Hallie about the call.

A wave of sultry air assaulted Mona as she opened the apartment door and stepped inside. Oscar was waiting at the door, his fat body swaying in countermotion to his wagging tail. Mona lifted him into her arms and nuzzled her face into the dog's neck, then shifted him to her hip and walked across the room. She stopped in front of her mother's rocker near the dresser, running her free hand across the detailed carving of the back.

"Exceedingly abundantly above all we ask or think. That's what You've promised. And You know all the things I'm asking that are most precious to my heart, don't You?" she spoke softly.

Behind her, a voice laughed. "So Oscar's a psychic?"

She turned. Hallie leaned in the doorway, her hair frosted with wood dust and her fingers streaked with stain.

"I wasn't talking to Oscar; I was talking to God. I haven't done enough praying lately, and I feel like the air has gone out of my soul."

Hallie stepped inside the room. "I didn't seem to hear Him say anything back to you, now, did I?" She waved a hand wildly in front of her face. "And talk about suffocating, it's hot enough up here to gag a maggot. Are you coming back down?"

"In a minute. I came up to get Oscar out of this heat and to pick up a few things."

Hallie shifted her weight, and her eyes shot to the floor as she shoved her hands into the pockets of her shorts. Mona knew the look—a look of guilt.

"Something on your mind, Hal?"

Hallie's head jerked up, her eyes widened, and something flickered there that Mona couldn't quite recognize.

"Not a thing. You looking for anything I can help you find?"

Mona searched her niece's face, but the look had passed. "Actually, I came up to get something I've been wanting to give to you."

She plopped Oscar unceremoniously on the bed and reached for the purse she'd placed on the floor near the rocker. Rummaging for a moment, she pulled something from its depths, then held her hands behind her back as she crossed the room to where Hallie stood.

"I know this is a small thing, Hallie. Something silly, actually, but when I saw this the other day at a yard sale, I wanted you to have it, but I want to tell you why."

Mona drew a hand from behind her back and pulled Hallie's hands from her pockets, clasping her cold, stained fingers in her own, then placing the tiny, die-cast motorcycle in them. Hallie's head was bent as she stared at her hands, and Mona fought off the urge to lift her chin so she could see her niece's eyes. Her voice was soft as she continued.

"I think you decided to look for something the day you took your dad's bike and came to the beach house. I think you were hoping to find a way to forgive yourself because you thought that forgiving yourself would bring you peace. But God wanted you to find more than that when you ran away that day. He wanted you to find Him. You'll never find peace until you find Him. He's chasing you, Hal, and you can keep on running, or you can turn around and fall into His arms. I promise He'll catch you. And I promise that if you keep on running, you'll never find forgiveness or peace. But I think that you already know that."

Hallie's hands trembled for a moment.

Please, God, open the eyes of her heart.

Minutes seemed to pass, but Mona was aware only of the pleading of her own heart and the trembling of Hallie's icy hands. Then slowly, the fingers closed around the metal figure and constricted tightly until beads of blood oozed from Hallie's palm.

"Hallie!" Mona grabbed the blood-stained hand and pried the fingers apart, forcing them straight until she could grasp the figure and wrench it from Hallie's fist. Her eyes flew to her niece's face, but there were no tears.

"You don't know what I've done, Aunt Mona." The voice was steely.

"And you don't know what I've done, Hallie. Or what Elsie's done, or my pastor, or the man who pumps gas down the street for a living. None of us ever sees a fraction of our sin, because we're too blind to see what sin really is and how it grieves the heart of God."

Mona struggled to keep her voice even.

"Do you think your sins are so great they cancel out God's desire to save you? What about the father who deserts his children or the pastor who has an affair? Or maybe the girl who sells her body on the street corner or the felon on death row? Who put you in charge of drawing the lines of God's grace? Are you so self-centered that you've drawn a circle just around yourself, or have you also taken on the job of deciding who in the rest of the world is worth saving? The truth is we're all prostitutes and felons and not one of us is worthy."

Mona stroked her hands across Hallie's until the tiny blood droplets stained her own palms.

"We're all that loved, Hal. No matter who we are, no matter what we've done. You just need to give yourself permission to believe it."

Everything in Mona's head screamed for her to keep talking until the emptiness in Hallie's eyes was gone. But everything in her heart told her to walk away.

Mona placed the toy back in Hallie's hands, cupped her niece's chin, and drew her close.

Please, God, help her see herself how You see her. Loved. Forgiven. Free. Help me see my father the same way.

Hallie's eyes stared back into her own. There were no tears, just a reflection of terror, the terror of a heart's first glimpse of its own strangulating lies illuminated by the power of truth.

"I'd do anything for you, Hallie, but I can't do this. This is just you and God."

Mona lifted a corner of her shirt and brushed the blood from Hallie's skin. The flow had slowed to a pinprick. Then she kissed her gently on the forehead and walked out the door.

Mona didn't remember walking to the park or the looks of those who passed her and glanced at her blood-stained shirt. And she didn't remember the prayers that poured from her as she huddled at the base of the huge oak tree near the mill pond.

What she did remember was the terror that had spilled from Hallie's eyes. Terror that had replaced the anger and told her that, for the first time since Stacy had died, perhaps Hallie was facing the truth.

Chapter Sixteen

It was nearly suppertime when Mona returned to the shop. Elsie had brought back enough food to make even the massive trestle table call out for mercy, and she seemed oblivious to the tension that hung in the air as she transferred a growing mountain of Tupperware bowls from her vintage Grand Marquis to the table. With something decidedly less than tact, Hallie had announced at lunch that she was dying for homemade macaroni and cheese with bacon, and that Mona's version made from Kraft and Bac-Os reminded her too much of hospital food. Knowing full well she'd been manipulated, Elsie had glowed in the affirmation of her culinary skills and prepared a bathtub full of the cheesy casserole, along with buckets of sweet coleslaw, baked beans, steaming corn on the cob, and key lime pie.

But Hallie's mood had soured. The girl who had conversed so affably with Harold at lunch had been swallowed by a belligerent, stone-faced teenager. She'd scarfed down two plates, careful to hide her discreetly bandaged hand, then clomped up to the apartment and buried her face in a book. Elsie left shortly after the table had been cleared, airing her opinion of ungrateful teenagers to the world at large as the door to the alley slammed behind her, leaving Mona to face an evening of sullen silences on her own.

It wasn't until after breakfast the next day that Mona remembered Elsie's surprise, as Hallie banged in and out the back door, hauling out the Meijer bags that held her belongings and stowing them in the truck. Mona sat at the office desk, making notes for Elsie, notes she knew would be ignored even as she wrote them. The ledger still occupied the center of the desk, but she refused to open it again. It would be there when she got back.

She checked her watch: 8:20. She was all too aware that time was slipping away, precious time she needed with Hallie. God had certainly made the sun stand still for Joshua, but she wasn't sure she had the faith to ask Him to do it again. She struggled with the rising panic growing within her and reminded herself of the truth. This struggle wasn't about telling Hallie the right thing the right way. It was about Hallie listening to the voice of God stirring in her own heart.

God, create a maelstrom in this child's soul if You need to. Break through to her before her parents come to take her away.

She willed the anger from her thoughts, anger that Ellen had once again broken a promise to her daughter.

And give me grace, Lord, not some feeling I try to muster up on my own. Give me Your love for Ellen and Phil and the vision to see who You created them to be.

The back door slammed. Mona recognized the padding footfalls and looked up. Elsie was slipping past the office door, carrying a brown cardboard carton, atop which rested a smaller box wrapped in pale blue paper.

"Just finishing up in here, Els," Mona called out as she rose from her chair and headed into the shop. Her fingers flickered across her cheek as she crossed the threshold, and she quickly shoved her hand into her pocket as she paused at the end of the trestle table and eyed the storage box. It was identical to the many Hallie had dragged down from the apartment storage closet to her office to sort.

Hallie drifted in from the back room, and Mona noted the circles under her eyes that betrayed the tossing and turning she had heard from the bed on the foldout love seat during the night. Hallie was wearing her new jeans and a West Shore High School T-shirt that had apparently been pulled from Mona's drawer.

"Set yourselves down, the two of you," Elsie commanded.

That morning's fashion inspiration had apparently been patriotic, Mona observed. White slacks and red tennis shoes were paired with a red, white, and blue striped shirt with embroidered gold stars across the chest. Even Elsie's nails had been freshly painted a bright red.

"Hallie Bowen, don't go makin' that face at me. Get your bottom in that chair there."

She pointed at a mission-style oak rocker as she gestured Mona onto a Victorian settee next to it. Like a child, Mona did as she was told.

"I got somethin' here for each of you, but I need your promise that you won't go peekin' until you're back at the beach house, and you won't go openin' nothin' unless you're together."

Elsie's cheeks were flushed, and Mona thought she read a glimpse of excitement in her expression.

"You promise, or I haul these back to my car faster'n you can spit a nickel."

Hallie glanced at Mona, an uncertain expression on her face, and Mona raised her eyebrows in response.

"I guess we can promise, can't we, Hallie?" Mona smiled.

Elsie's hands flew to her hips.

"I know you, Mona VanderMolen. You been openin' your Christmas presents and tapin' 'em back up since you was three. I need your word here. From your mouth to God's own ear."

They promised—Mona out of respect and Hallie out of simple fear. But they both knew that if either one of them broke their promise, they would live to regret it, and the entire village of Stewartville would know they were cheaters.

So between Hallie's sullen silence and the suspense of Elsie's surprise, it was a long ride back to the beach house.

Hallie carried the boxes into the living room and placed them on the floor near the slider to the deck as Mona had asked. They'd spoken little on the way home, and Mona had once again deferred to music to fill the uncomfortable silence between them. She'd spent most of the drive to Muskegon in prayer. It was obvious Hallie was still running. The stony silence had told her so. From the moment she'd crawled into the truck, Hallie had huddled in a corner, her face turned toward the window, her eyes closed. The moment they'd arrived at the beach house, she'd placed the boxes in the living room and had disappeared into the bathroom, locking the door behind her.

Mona stood at the slider to the deck and basked in the view of the rolling waters of Lake Michigan, knowing she needed to feel anew the sense of wonder it always evoked in her. Wonder for the greatness of a God who chose to create such stunning beauty. Wonder for the greatness of a God who chose to love His broken children with such stunning beauty. Whitecaps glistened on the three-foot crests that broke on the beach in swirls and eddies of infinite variety. She stood in the silence as an awareness of God's love washed over her.

She knew that each wave that broke was one less moment with Hallie, one moment closer to Ellen's arrival. Her hand rose to her neck, and she fingered the ring that hung from the chain. God's sovereignty and man's freedom to act—she knew the paradox, the apparent contradiction. But she also knew she didn't need to understand the mystery—she only needed to listen to the voice of the Spirit who would guide her. She turned and directed her words toward the closed bathroom door.

"We need a celebration today, Hallie. I think that's what Elsie wanted."

She waited, the ring still clasped in her left hand.

"How about lunch on the beach and an opening ceremony? It's only ten thirty, so you can have an hour or so to veg out in the sun. Then we'll go all out with peanut butter and jelly sandwiches, maybe a frozen Snickers bar or two. Sounds like a plan to me, so why don't you get changed while I run out for just a bit?"

Her throat grew suddenly tight, and she let the ring fall from her fingers again to her chest. She didn't wait for Hallie's reply before she slipped out the door and toward the beach.

Her feet were heavy as she walked across the dune toward Gilead, her legs feeling the soft sand give way beneath her steps as she pushed forward. A walk through a mile of dune sand was equal to four or five miles on packed dirt. Locals who wanted a real workout didn't run the beaches, they hiked the gentle lakeside mountains that shifted under the unremitting offshore winds. Mona felt the strain in her calves and slowed her pace. She knew her wisdom with Hallie had long since been exhausted. Each step was moving them farther apart, and tomorrow Hallie would be gone. She paused and stood for a moment at the wood-railed walkway as tears slipped down her face, praying that amid the outstretched arms of the trees she would find the whisper of God's voice.

God, let me hear You, if hearing You is what's best. And if what is best is the silence, let me hear You even in that.

She wiped the tears and climbed slowly.

The sounds of the surf breaking on the beach enveloped her as she made her way. It took only minutes to ascend the familiar boardwalk paths and stairs through the dunes that led to the refuge she had sought so often since Stacy died. And it took only seconds to read the sign on the door of the Prayer Tower and feel her heart drop.

Occupied.

For a moment, it felt as if a door in her own heart had slammed shut. But she whispered the truth to herself. It didn't matter where she was or what she said. God would be there to hear her. He had already heard her.

She turned and sat on a wooden bench near the door to wait, resting her elbows on her knees and cradling her head in her hands as the words formed in her heart and poured from her lips. Tears came, but she didn't hold them back. She knew that the tears spoke the longings of her heart most clearly. The moments drifted away as she wept and prayed, enfolded by the sounds of the wind and the waves.

Time touched eternity as she sat beneath the trees. Her only awareness was of her heart overwhelmed by the heart of God.

A sound tugged at the perimeter of her thoughts, and she pushed it away, the sound of a door opening and gently closing. A growing sense of presence invaded her awareness, and she whispered a final word and raised her head.

Adam Dean was staring at her. For a moment, she wasn't sure where she was or why he was there. She didn't know how long she stared back.

Recovering, she brushed away the tears and stood, searching for the right words as she glanced around.

"Adam, what a surprise."

He nodded. "I'd have to agree."

He cleared his throat, and a look flickered across his face—of anger? Pity? Mona couldn't be sure. He was immaculate in crisply creased navy chinos and a white polo shirt embroidered with *Dean's Distinctive Reproductions* on the left breast. He cleared his throat once again, apparently at a loss for words.

Mona was suddenly aware that she was gritty and wind-blown from the drive, her face streaked with tears and who knew what else. She tried to cover one bare foot with the other as she searched for words. This time it was too important. It would be her last chance to put things right if she could just think before she spoke.

"I'm not stalking you. Really. I have a house just down the beach, and I come here a lot."

She shifted her weight and gestured vaguely toward the beach house. Adam continued to stare.

"The sign on the door said 'occupied,' so I thought I'd wait. I didn't want to disturb someone who might be praying. I actually can be polite sometimes."

She felt something on her cheek and took a swipe at a tear that had escaped.

Adam rummaged in his pants pocket and then extended his hand to her.

"I was hoping for a Kleenex, but I guess this is all I can muster."

She took it and smiled. It was a breath mint.

"I hope you'll forgive me if I don't wipe my face with it."

He smiled, and suddenly the laugh wrinkles were there again.

"I'm afraid you're the one who needs to forgive me, Mona. I'm not sure this is the time or the place, but I want you to know I'm ashamed of the way I spoke to you the other day. I'd appreciate the opportunity to stop by sometime in the next day or so to make an appropriate apology. I don't want to keep you from . . ." He gestured lamely toward the Prayer Tower door.

Mona heard the sound of voices approaching on the stairway, but she willed herself to hold his gaze.

"Prayer. I come here for prayer. And that would be fine, Adam. I have my own apology all prepared. In fact, I tried to call you several times to deliver it, but you didn't seem to be available. Not that I blame you. But I also wanted to ask you something else."

"Something else?"

The sound of the voices grew louder, children laughing and a mother calling out.

"Yes, something else. I need to ask you about the chair, the rocker. Did you send it to me? And why . . . why would you do that?"

Footsteps reverberated on the wooden walkway, and through the trees, the sound of a woman's laughter drifted toward them. Mona glanced in the direction of the voice for a moment, then back at Adam.

There was deliberation in his voice as he spoke.

"I believe that family is one of God's greatest gifts to us, or at least it should be. I also know it doesn't work out that way for everybody. The chair seemed important to you, to your sense of family, so I thought it was important for you to have it, a lot more important than my having it. I bought it a few years ago at an estate sale in Muskegon because I thought it was a beautiful piece, and I've made a few copies of it. Now I can give it back to you. That's all."

She swallowed, a knot forming in her throat.

"You can't possibly know how much it means to me. There's no way I can thank you. I don't think anyone has ever done anything this kind for me before . . . really." The words fell away, and Mona suddenly found herself staring into Adam's deep brown eyes.

He lowered his head and slid his hands into his pockets.

"I know what it's like to love someone and lose them and to be left only with memories and a few of the things they touched." He raised his head. "And you're more than welcome."

A toddler careened around a bend in the walkway, followed by a young woman in hot pursuit, clutching the hand of what appeared to be a twin. Mona dodged out of their path. Behind them, more voices rose from the wooden walkway.

"It looks like I'll be taking my prayers somewhere a bit more serene today," she said, gesturing in the direction of her house. "The tower's my favorite place, but it seems to be everyone else's today, too. I'd better be heading back. Hallie and I have a date for lunch on the beach."

Adam nodded. "And I've got a meeting with the conference director. I guess we'll have to save those apologies for another time." He smiled and extended his hand. "I think congratulations are in order."

Mona looked at him quizzically as she reached to shake his hand. "Because?"

Adam smiled, and once again, Mona noted the crinkles.

"We've just had our first conversation without an argument."

His hand gripped hers as the words echoed in her mind.

Our first conversation. Perhaps there would be others.

Hallie carried Elsie's boxes from the living room to the beach, dancing gingerly across the hot sand, and placed them carefully in the center of the faded sheet Mona had taken from the storage shed and spread in the hollow of a small dune. Then they returned to the house and piled paper plates with fresh fruit salad and peanut butter and jelly sandwiches before they returned and settled themselves side-by-side, facing the boxes and the blue-green expanse of Lake Michigan. Hallie popped a strawberry into her mouth with her fingers. Apparently the anticipation of opening the boxes had lightened her mood.

"I'm starving," she mumbled through the food. "And where on earth did you disappear to? I was worried sick about you! You could at least have the courtesy to tell me where you're going before you run off."

Mona saw the smile.

"Very funny. You were sucking up the rays while I was gone, flirting with every guy that walked past. And if you must know, I needed a few minutes to myself before we talked."

Hallie's hand froze above her plate.

"Before we talked?"

Mona reached into a plastic bucket of ice, pulled out a Diet Coke, and popped the tab.

"Later," she said firmly. "We're talking later. Right now we're eating lunch and opening boxes. I, for one, have waited long enough to see what Elsie's diabolical mind has cooked up. So, who goes first?"

She leaned forward and pulled the boxes closer. Hallie responded by snatching the pale blue package from the top of the carton and ripping off the envelope taped to the top.

"Good heavens, child, you act like it's the first

present you've ever gotten. And read the note out loud, or I'll just have to read it myself later when you're not looking."

Mona waited, watching intently as Hallie's eyes scanned the few spidery lines scrawled across the notebook paper.

"So? You're killing me with suspense, girl."

Hallie swallowed, then slowly read.

"God gives us a fresh page each and every day, Hallie. This is for your next page and many more to come. Choose carefully what you write. Love, Elsie McFeeney."

Mona felt her heart go still as Hallie looked up at her, but she was smiling.

"I know what it is. It's a diary."

She tore back the paper and lifted the lid on the small box. A red leather diary lay nestled in the tissue paper. Hallie lifted it out, slid back a small gold button, and leafed through the pages. On the inside cover, Elsie had written, *To Hallie with love, on the first day of the rest of your life.*

The waves broke on the beach in a gentle cadence as Mona silently waited. She watched as a piece of driftwood floated in on the surf and rested for a moment in the sand before the next wave drew it back into the swirling water.

Please, God, please. A smile, a crack in the armor—anything!

"I like it." Hallie spoke quietly as she stared at the book in her hands. "A whole lot, I think."

Mona felt herself exhale.

"Now yours," Hallie said as she pulled an envelope from the top of the carton and handed it to Mona.

Mona carefully tore it open and unfolded the paper. The note was long, and her eyes swept the page as she scanned the contents.

"No fair," Hallie said. "Read it out loud, the whole thing."

Mona skimmed the page as words leaped into her consciousness.

Brown sweater . . . daddy . . . passing them on.

She cleared her throat and glanced up at Hallie, fear growing in her heart and her chest tightening. For a moment, it felt as if the air had been sucked from her lungs.

How had Elsie known?

"It's okay, Aunt Mona. It's from Elsie. Trust her. She wanted us to do this together, so trust me too."

The word shot through Mona's heart like a knife.

Trust.

The voice whispered in her heart.

Trust me too.

She turned toward Hallie and spoke softly, the words coming haltingly as she watched a strand of hair dance across her sunburned cheeks.

"I trust Elsie and I trust you because I know your hearts. If this box is what I think it is, Elsie knew it held things I wanted to hide away, and she knew I needed you here right now to help me open it because it was going to be hard. So I need you to help me. Can you do that for me, Hallie?"

Mona kissed her fingertips, planted them on Hallie's heart, and waited for the response. It came in an instant, as Hallie raised her bandaged hand, kissed her fingertips, and covered Mona's fingers.

Mona drew a deep breath and began to read:

Dear Mona,

I found these when Hallie and I were sorting boxes this week. At first, I thought it was just clothes, because there was an old brown sweater of your father's on top. I think it must have been his because he's wearing it in most every picture I ever saw of him and your mama. I found these under the sweater, and I knew you needed to have them.

I think your daddy has something to say to you that maybe he didn't know how to say when he was alive. I hope it's okay that I'm passing his thoughts on to you this way, with Hallie there and all. It just seemed best.

Love,
Elsie

Mona felt her heart stop as she stared at the words. Her instincts had been right. She knew what was in the box. She had packed it herself and shoved it to the back of her closet years ago, hoping to forget it forever.

The sensation in her chest tightened, and for a moment she wondered if she might pass out. She felt the warmth of Hallie's body as she inched closer.

"You gotta breathe, Aunt Mona, or you're gonna keel over right here, and no matter how good you look for your age, I'm not doing mouth-to-mouth on you."

Mona swatted at Hallie's leg and breathed deeply for several moments. Then she leaned forward and slipped the lid from the carton.

The box was exactly as she remembered. Her father's brown cardigan sweater lay folded neatly on the top. She lifted it gently and handed it to Hallie. Beneath the sweater lay dozens of small leather-bound books of varying shades.

Hallie leaned forward and peered in.

"What are they?"

Mona sighed and closed her eyes for a moment.

"Diaries. My father's diaries. He kept them from as far back as I can remember."

"Have you read them?"

"No."

"Not any?"

"No."

"You're kidding. You've had them all these years and haven't even read a page?"

"No!"

Immediately, Mona regretted her tone. She glanced at Hallie, but she hadn't seemed to notice. She was reaching into the box and piling the books gently in the sand.

"Look at this—1945. He was in the war then, right? And here's 1952, 1953. Hey look, 1960. Isn't that the year you were born? You mean you never wanted to read what he wrote on the day you were born?"

Mona swallowed hard, the pressure in her chest now a hard ball.

"If you must know, I've never read any of them because I've spent most of my life mad at my father. He was a hard man, sometimes a cruel man, and I never wanted to know anything more about him than I thought I knew growing up. It just seemed easier. But the older I get, the more I realize that my memories were a child's memories, and maybe I didn't know him after all. Or maybe what I knew was just a small part. Maybe there's something more I'm supposed to know."

She reached for the diary marked 1960 and stroked the cover between her hands.

"I'm just like you, Hallie. I chose to believe a lie. I believed some people and some things weren't worth forgiving."

She turned and leveled tear-filled eyes at her niece.

"I was wrong."

Hallie turned away and began slowly replacing the books in the box, but Mona rested a hand on her arm.

"Hal, these diaries . . . today . . . this isn't an accident. Just like my mother's chair wasn't an accident. It's part of God's plan. I'm asking you to do something for me, something that's important, the most important thing I've asked anybody to do in a long time.

"I've been a hypocrite, Hallie. I've preached to you about forgiving yourself when I've refused to forgive my father. But by God's grace, I'm going to forgive him. Maybe it's something I'm going to have to learn to do a little at a time, but I'm going to start. I want to put my father's ring on my chain with my mother's ring tonight. I want to do it at the pier when the sun is setting and make it something that will honor him. I'm asking you to keep my dad's ring for me until then."

Hallie's face went white, and she dropped a book in the sand. "I . . . I don't think I can."

"Of course you can." Mona squeezed her arm. "I know you can. And you know it, too. You already have the ring. You took it from my jewelry box in Stewartville, probably when you were in my room bringing down boxes. No, it's okay to look at me.

And it's okay that you did it, Hal. I just need to know why."

Hallie had drawn her knees to her chin and wrapped her arms around her legs. Her voice shook as she spoke, staring over the water to the horizon. Mona stroked her arm gently.

"I never wanted to take anything from you, Aunt Mona. You know that."

"Then why, Hallie?" Mona asked softly.

"I don't know! I guess the ring proved to me that you were angry, and it was all right to be angry if you were angry. It told me it was all right to hate somebody, even if it was myself. I didn't think you wanted it anyway. You didn't want it, did you?"

For a moment, a wordless horror shot through Mona as she realized what she had done. She had fed the very lie that was consuming Hallie's heart. She had fed it with her own lies and her own self-deception. The truth slammed into her soul, and she felt as if she would crumble beneath the weight.

Mona gathered Hallie in her arms and felt the tremble of her shoulders as she rocked her silently. The diary fell in the sand between them, and she shot wordless prayers heavenward. She stroked Hallie's hair like a child and stroked her back until the sobs subsided. It was a long time before Mona could find words.

"Hallie, I can't tell you how broken I am for the

way my anger infected you, even when I was too blind to see it. God knows, I'm so sorry. It's because of you that truth finally has broken through my anger and showed me that forgiving my father is a choice. Forgiveness is always a choice, Hal. And it's a choice I'm making tonight, in front of you. With you. I'm making you my ring-bearer. Then tonight, when we're out at the pier, I'll give you the second gift I have for you. One I've been saving."

Mona hoped the words would bring a response, but she was wrong. They sat beneath the warming rays of the sun until the heat grew scorching. Still silent, Hallie gathered up the paper plates and her diary and headed back to the house. A moment later Mona carefully repacked the box, replaced the lid, and followed her.

But she slipped one volume into the pocket of her shorts before she turned to follow Hallie into the shade of the house.

The cover read *1960.*

Chapter Seventeen

Mona chose her favorite swimming spot, inside the arms of the two breakwater piers at Pere Marquette Park. Before they'd left the house, she'd stepped out onto the deck and taken note of the daunting waves, cresting at four feet in the steady offshore winds. She knew the surf would be gentler on the section of beach protected by the wide, L-shaped pier on the south side of the channel and the North Muskegon breakwater on the far side. It was often a quieter stretch of sand, down the sidewalk and around a small dune from the beach volleyball courts where a dozen or so nets were strung for the hundreds of players who gathered for pick-up games and tournaments throughout the summer. But Mona prayed for solitude more than quiet surf as she and Hallie made their way down the sidewalk through clusters of dozing parents, sand-encrusted children, and bronzed teenagers.

Only a handful of volleyball games were underway, mostly high school and college kids scrimmaging in a tangle of tanned limbs. Hallie was the first to spot Dan. He stood in the serving position on the team nearest the water and waved briefly in their direction before delivering an ace, low and fast.

Mona chose to swim before the sun dipped lower on the horizon, throwing her towel and tote bag in a heap on the beach and running headlong into the surf, knowing Hallie would lag behind. The water was colder than she'd expected, and she drew in a breath and braced for the shock.

Never wade. Just face the cold and get it over with.

The words washed through her mind as she dove and sliced through the water, stretching toward the sandy bottom beneath her. Words her father had spoken to her. Words she'd found herself repeating to the girls their first summer with her at the beach house. Stacy had always been the wader, inching her way into the waves while her sister had raced ahead and plunged into the oncoming waves. But that had been before.

Mona stood and scanned the shallow water behind her. Hallie stood thigh-deep in the rolling surf, her hands extended outward from her sides like a tightrope walker. Mona watched her for a moment and waved, then turned back toward deeper water.

She stroked slowly for a few yards, then turned and floated on her back beyond the breaking surf, the muffled sounds of the beach obscured by the undulating curtain of water. She closed her eyes and felt the warmth of the sun on her face as her body rose and fell with the swells.

Like being rocked in the hand of God, she thought.

She drifted in the watery embrace, her hands fanning the surface in graceful arcs, her hair splaying out about her head like a crimson sunburst. The moments slipped away, marked only by the rising and falling of the swells.

The water cupped her chin and tickled her ears, stroking her thoughts into a wordless, hovering peace. A hand touched her shoulder, and Mona opened her eyes. Hallie stood neck-deep in the water beside her.

"I'm going in. I thought I'd sit on the beach for a while and see if Dan comes by, maybe invite him to the house later tonight, unless you're planning something you haven't told me about. I don't suppose you'd do that, would you?"

Mona blinked away the water that was dripping from her sodden hair. Hallie's eyes were narrowed, and her mouth was drawn in a straight line. The question couldn't have been a coincidence.

From the shore a voice called out, and they both turned to look. Dan stood, waving, beside a pile of towels and the sheet that Hallie had spread.

"I guess we'll just have to save that question for later," Hallie said flatly. Then she turned and half-walked, half-swam back toward the beach as Mona watched.

She knows, an inner voice told her.

Mona fought back the urge to follow. Something in her spirit told her to wait. The time wasn't right, and her heart knew it. She eased onto her back again and gave in to the rhythm of the waves as the sun burned into her face and the voice stirred once more.

Trust Me. She's Mine.

Mona spun her hands in gentle circles as the water licked her face, leaving only her eyes, nose, and mouth exposed above the surface. Velvet vibrations of sound thrummed in the water as she drifted on the edge of consciousness. She gave in to the pulse of the waves as they lifted and lowered her in their steady rhythm.

Her mind drifted to the dream in hazy swirls of consciousness, the dream of her mother bobbing and waving. But among the images, flashes of reality, of real memories. Memories of her mother kneeling in newly turned soil, planting crimson geraniums. Of her mother smoothing wrinkles from freshly washed sheets as she folded them. Of her mother rocking slowly, her hands lightly resting on the pages of a Bible.

Then a new image came—of her father standing behind her mother as she rocked, his hand resting lightly on her shoulder.

One by one, new pictures washed over her mind with a brilliance that stirred something deep within her, and Mona smiled, her hands tracing gentle swaths that radiated outward from her fingers. But like the flicker of a neon sign, the dream returned, beckoning her into its recesses as the brilliant memories faded. Seconds stretched into minutes as Mona hovered at the edge of the dream until the voice within her stirred again.

Choose.

Bitterness or forgiveness. Truth or a lie.

For the first time since the nightmares had come, Mona realized that it was not about choosing after all. It was about giving up.

The dream washed over her again, and this time

she embraced it, giving shape to the vision, choosing its colors.

From the shore, a man in a brown sweater called to her, his words blurred, but his tone welcoming.

The voice of her father, a loving voice.

She waited as his words rang out a second time, clear and forceful.

I've always loved you, Mona. Always.

I know, Dad.

In that moment, the truth flooded her mind, the truth that forgiveness shapes our vision of those we forgive, the truth that forgiveness would shape her from that moment on.

The dream was gone, and the sunlight overhead bored through her closed lids. For a moment, the burning heat was almost more than she could bear. Then she opened her eyes.

She rolled over and scanned the beach as the waves lifted and lowered her in the rolling surf. Dan sat on a towel in the hollow of the dune, and Hallie was behind him, slipping shorts and a tank top over her wet suit as she spoke. Mona waved in their direction, then headed to shore with slow, easy strokes. Words reverberated in her mind with each thrust of her arms.

I forgive you, Dad. And I'm going to look for the scattered seeds of your love in my life and claim them.

Minutes later, swathed in a beach towel, she

dropped into the sand beside Hallie and Dan and extended her long legs as her toes scooped sand over her feet.

"It was a great swim, Hallie. Absolutely amazing. Hello, Dan, it's good to see you."

But what had seemed to be an animated conversation moments before had gone silent. There was a pause before Hallie spoke.

"Dan was just asking me when I'm heading home, Aunt Mona. For a minute I thought you'd let him in on your secret, but I guess I was wrong. I saw you run upstairs yesterday to take a call, and I listened at the door while Elsie was busy in the back room. Apparently, it's the only way I can get information about my own life."

Mona felt Hallie's eyes boring into her own.

"I'm guessing from the way you've been acting today that it's probably tomorrow. And I was thinking of adding the part where I tell Dan that this would make about the ten-millionth promise to me that my parents have broken. And then I was going to tell him how ticked I am because you apparently didn't plan on telling me at all, even though this afternoon you were giving me a grand lecture about trust. Oh, yeah, and I was going to add that I really don't give a rip anyway. That's pretty much it."

Hallie's tone was dead, and Mona felt as if she'd been slapped. Her eyes burned, and she blinked hard. She hadn't let herself think about tomorrow.

But Hallie was right: she hadn't trusted her not to run, not to do something stupid. It had seemed too risky, and she'd refused to think about the price she might pay for Hallie's feelings of betrayal. Now she was paying that price.

"Hallie, I'm sorry. Your mom did call yesterday and tell me they're coming for you tomorrow morning. I should have told you, but I wanted to protect you as long as possible. I decided to wait until after tonight so we could enjoy one last evening together. It was a bad decision, and I was wrong. I'm sorry. Please forgive me for not telling you the truth as soon as I knew it."

Mona turned toward Dan, sensing his tension.

"Forgive me for putting you in an embarrassing situation like this. I wanted the time we had together to last as long as possible without any . . . any of this." Her hand rose and fell to her side limply.

Dan rose and brushed the sand from his shorts.

"No apology necessary, Miss VanderMolen. But I think I'd better leave you two alone. I pulled an eight-hour shift guarding today and then came down here for a little volleyball, so I'm pretty done in. Maybe I'll stop by tomorrow morning to say good-bye, if that's all right."

Mona watched from the corner of her eye as Hallie dropped her head and began tracing circles in the sand.

"Of course, Dan. I know Hallie's parents would

love to meet you. And I'm sure she'd like to say a more appropriate good-bye. I know this is awkward, and it's my fault."

Dan shook his head. "I'll stop by in the morning with some of my mother's muffins, and we can say good-bye then."

He rested a hand briefly on the top of Hallie's wet curls, then strode off around the dune toward the parking lot.

Mona ignored Hallie's icy silence as she quickly dried her arms and legs and slipped a beach cover-up over her head. She slid her hand into a deep pocket of the terry cloth robe and felt until her fingers touched the box. It was there.

"Do you think you can stand me long enough to walk to the lighthouse?"

Hallie's head was still down, her fingers moving woodenly in the sand.

"I don't remember a lot of good times between my mom and dad, Hallie, so this is a special place to me. It's one of the few places about family. If my mom and dad had a special place, maybe this was it. So it'll mean a lot to me, Hal, to have you with me today, in this place. But it will mean even more to know you forgive me."

Hallie gave the sand a firm pat, then raised her head. The anger had drained from her face, and Mona saw only the eyes of a frightened child.

"I'm mad because I have to go. You know that."

"Yes."

"And I'm mad because I want to run, but there's nowhere to go. I'm not ready to go home now, not yet."

Mona waited.

"There's nowhere else to run, do you understand that?" Her voice was a strangled whisper.

Hallie stared at the horizon as a rivulet of water dribbled from her jaw and jerked its way slowly down her arm in a path of fits and starts. Then she turned and extended her hand, and Mona reached down and pulled her to her feet as they stood eye-to-eye.

"There's never anywhere to run when you're running from what's inside, Hal. I know because I've been running, too. I'm through running tonight, Hal, from my anger at my father. I've confessed it, and God Himself can't remember it anymore. I wish you could know the freedom I feel, knowing I can think of the man who hurt me so much and not see just the pain anymore.

"My dad was a Christian. Mom told me she was sure of it, even though he didn't seem to know how to put feet on it. But I want to see my dad the way Jesus saw him—not just the broken mess, but the beauty of His creation, of His image in him."

Mona felt the pressure on her fingers, hard and tight, as Hallie squeezed them.

"His image, even in broken, messed-up people?"

"Even in broken, messed-up people."

They were the first words of hope Mona had heard from Hallie since Stacy's death.

"People like you and people like me."

Mona brushed the sand from her hands and gave Hallie a quick hug. Then they slowly set out toward the pier together.

The wide concrete walkway stretched out into the lake for a quarter mile, ending at the red lighthouse that marked the southern arm of the inlet to the Muskegon Lake Channel. A dozen or so people walked ahead of them on the narrow ribbon of concrete that pierced the surging expanse of water. It was a destination that had drawn generations to stand in its towering presence—lovers, parents, daredevils, those on the brink of joy, and those on the brink of despair.

A few yards in front of them, a young couple walking hand-in-hand stopped to embrace and whisper. Mona encircled Hallie's waist with her arm and drew her to the side of the ten-foot-wide pier as the couple silently walked past them. Mona fingered the box in her pocket, running her fingers across the lid as she lifted her voice above the sound of the wind and the waves. Their pace slowed.

"The nightmare is about Stacy drowning, isn't it?"

Mona watched the sun slipping toward the horizon. She waited. Hallie's steps had slowed to match her own as she stared toward the lighthouse. The words came more quickly than Mona had expected.

"It's like a tape that plays over and over in my head."

Her voice was trembling, and Mona took her hand and squeezed it.

"You were with us on the beach. You saw it. We were just swimming . . . and . . . and then she was gone."

Mona pulled Hallie closer and slipped her arm around her shoulder.

"Yes, that's true, Hal. But there's something else, the part you're afraid to tell me."

Mona waited, but Hallie didn't speak. Her eyes stared straight ahead.

"A necklace is always in your nightmare. I've heard your screams too many times not to know. I think it's the necklace I gave Stacy that weekend, exactly like the one I'd given you the summer before, made from stones from my mother's jewelry, the stones that spelled *dearest*. Am I right, Hal?"

They'd reached the point where the walkway narrowed to six feet and jutted to the northwest. Mona stopped and pulled Hallie into her arms. There was no resistance, but her body remained stiff and unyielding as Mona drew her close. In front of them, waves swirled and crashed in a manic choreography on the huge slabs of concrete piled against the pier for protection from the erosion of the pounding surf. The driving mist settled over Mona's head and shoulders in driving gusts and sent a shiver through her.

"Saying it out loud can't hurt you, Hallie."

The wind whipped the words away, the spray assaulting them in stinging pellets. A burst of water broke across the pier behind them, shooting a torrent to the far side of the walkway. On the pier ahead of them, a father with two small children turned and headed back to shore. A glance told Mona that everyone on the breakwater was leaving.

"I already know. Does that help?"

Hallie buried her face in Mona's chest, the words pouring out in a muffled jumble.

"I killed her. Is that what you need me to say? I took the necklace from her because I'd lost mine. I put it on that day just before we went down to the beach. And when we were swimming, she saw it and asked for it back, but I lied and said it was mine."

The shoulders convulsed with sobs that matched the writhing waves.

"She got mad and tried to take it, but I wouldn't let her. She was screaming at me, but you'd gone back to the house. And then she just grabbed for it, and the chain broke, and it slipped into the water."

Hallie's voice had become a whisper, and Mona could barely hear her over the wind and the surf. She bent her head.

"She dove down to get it, and she never came up again. I waited and waited. I kept thinking she'd come back up . . . that she was teasing me . . . but she didn't. She didn't . . . she never came . . . she never came . . ."

A choking sound rose from deep within Hallie, and for a moment Mona thought she would be sick. But the spasm eased as Mona stroked the convulsing shoulders and turned Hallie's face away from the gaze of people hurrying back toward shore and away from the pounding of the rising surf.

Minutes passed, and the weeping slowed. Gently, Mona took Hallie's shoulders, lifted her chin, and wiped the tears from her cheeks before she spoke.

"Hallie, you need to listen to me. You didn't kill Stacy by taking her necklace any more than I killed her by walking back to the house that day or your mother killed her by letting her come. You're not a murderer. That lie is chaining you to your past, and if you live in that lie, you'll never have a future. If your sister could speak to you right now, she'd tell you she loves you and that she's seen God face-to-face and there's nothing more wonderful than knowing Him. She would beg you to experience His forgiveness and love for yourself as one of His precious children."

The last of the people on the pier had scurried toward the safety of the beach, and they were alone. With an urgency that exploded from her soul, Mona prayed that her words would reach Hallie's heart. Deep within, she knew that time and eternity would touch in the next few moments, and one way or the other, Hallie's life would be changed forever.

"You told me once that, if you could have anything in the world, it would be a necklace, Stacy's necklace. If there's one thing your heart begs for, Hallie, it's to erase the past. God wants you to know that your past can't be erased, but it can be redeemed. He doesn't erase the mistakes of our past because He transforms them and redeems them, the same way He redeems and transforms us to become the people He created us to be. That's where the freedom lies."

Mona searched the tear-stained face, and the eyes that stared back into her own were searching. Her hand stirred in her pocket.

"This is your reminder of that truth, Hallie, the truth that God wants to redeem your pain, the truth that you are the dearest of His children, the truth that you are forgiven."

Mona pulled Hallie into her arms and buried her face in the mass of curls that billowed in the wind. One day soon, she would tell Hallie that she had spoken the words to herself, as well.

"I have a gift for you," she whispered.

Mona slipped the necklace from the box, then drew it slowly from her pocket. She'd worked into the night to repair the broken chain, and it lay draped between her fingers, the heart cradled in the palm of her hand.

"Lum found it in front of the beach house a week after we lost Stacy, and he thought it might belong to me. It's a gift from him. And from God."

A gust of wind drilled into them, and Mona braced herself, glancing up and down the pier. Even though they hadn't passed the bend in the outer arm of the breakwater, the waves were slapping at the concrete barricade with increasing intensity. They couldn't stay any longer.

Hallie stared. Then her hand moved slowly toward Mona's, and she fingered the chain lightly.

"You had another one made to look like it."

"That would make me a liar, Hal, and I've never lied to you."

Another wave rolled in, drenching them in its spray. Mona scanned the horizon and gauged the incoming clouds. The waves were continuing to rise, and the wind was gusting in unsteady gasps.

"We have to go back, Hallie. We can come out again at sunrise and walk to the lighthouse. It's not safe to be out here anymore."

Hallie pulled herself from Mona's arms. "Not until you put it on me. Please, Aunt Mona!"

Mona glanced at the incoming waves. The surf had risen to six feet. Her fingers tightened on the chain and she spun Hallie around, working the clasp as she lifted the damp, knotted hair from

Hallie's neck. In seconds, the necklace was secure and resting over Hallie's heart.

She turned to face Mona, tears streaming down her face as she stepped back and fingered the chain around her neck. Words formed on her lips, but Mona heard only the crashing of waves behind her, then a thunderous explosion as a geyser exploded over the breakwater in a torrent of fury, missing Hallie by inches.

Mona felt her legs give way as she was slammed to the pavement on the far edge of the walkway. The fury of the waves obliterated the sound of her skull cracking against the concrete. In a moment, a second wave swept her onto the rocks and wedged her between the jagged edges of two concrete slabs as the water roiled around her.

No one was there to hear the sound of Hallie's screams.

Chapter Eighteen

The swirling water rose and fell, straining to suck Mona beneath the surface with each cresting swell. She had landed between the ragged jaws of two rocks that tore at her flesh as the waves played tug-of-war with her body. Her limp arms flailed in the water without resistance, rising and falling in a surreal dance. In the moments when the unrelenting current released her, her head rested briefly on her chest before an incoming wave flung her back once more, cracking her skull against the slab that pinned her from behind.

A voice called out, but her eyes did not open, her head did not turn. Once again the voice called, and again she gave no response. She was intent, instead, on the shimmering gold and pink light that pulsated just beyond her. She strained to see, and a form slowly took shape before her eyes.

A woman in a pink terrycloth robe sitting cross-legged in an oversized flowerpot, busily crocheting a deep red afghan as the waves lifted, then lowered her with their swells.

A pulsating light emanated from behind Mona, matching its rhythm to the rhythm of the swells, its brightness increasing with the pull of each wave. Mona strained to work her shoulders free and inch her way forward, but the woman remained intent on her needlework.

The light burned into Mona's back, and the gold and pink shimmers glared in painful shards that pierced her eyes. The throbbing brightness engulfed her, and she squeezed her eyes tightly shut as pain ripped through her head.

The voice was louder now, the tone commanding. The woman in the flowerpot looked up from her knitting as she placed the needles gently in her lap. A corner of the afghan slipped into the water, and blood-red stains swirled out from it into the turbid waves. A hint of a smile played at the corners of her mouth as she locked her eyes on Mona's and extended her hand.

The deafening shriek of sirens slammed into Mona's ears. She turned toward the shore and saw her father standing beside the open door of an ambulance. He was calling, but his voice was drowned out by the roar of sirens. Mona watched, mesmerized, as his left hand beckoned slowly and glimmers of light flickered from his wedding band. Then he stepped into the water, the bloody waves swirling at his legs as he walked toward her.

Her hands slipped beneath the surface of the water as the current sucked at her legs and battered her arms. Her body was stiff and heavy, and a sudden coldness filled her chest as Hallie's face flickered before her, and her head slipped beneath the surface.

Mona.

I love you, Mom.

Mona.

I love you, Dad.

In the next moment, her mother and her father were beside her in the water, embracing her. The coldness left her body as together they sank, and the waves enfolded them all in a rainbow of pulsating light.

The glowing numbers of the alarm clock read 10:20 PM when the telephone awakened Elsie.

Tessa raised her head from her fleecy mat at the foot of the bed, and Oscar peeked his black nose from under the pink chenille bedspread. Elsie searched for her glasses as both animals began to whine.

It was almost as if they knew, she told friends later.

She stared into the darkness, straining to see as she listened in silence to the voice that spoke the heart-piercing words. Then she slowly placed the receiver back on the cradle and began to dress.

Ellen was standing in the bedroom, pouring the last drops from a crystal decanter when the tones of a cell phone invaded her thoughts. Thoughts of Phil, who had just slammed out the door. Thoughts of the woman he was escaping to, this time for good.

She willed herself to ignore the noise, but by the third ring, she was beaten like she'd been beaten by so many other threads of life she'd struggled to keep from unraveling. Too much of the unknown lay at the other end of an unanswered phone. It was impossible to screen out the sound that had tormented her since the day Mona had called to tell her Stacy was dead.

She glanced at the diamond-studded Gucci Phil had given her for their tenth anniversary as she walked to the delicate French desk near the window and picked up the phone. Ten thirty-five.

She squinted to read the name and number on the caller ID.

A Muskegon area code. Her hand trembled as she pressed the button to answer. The sound of wracking sobs rose to her ear, a familiar sound.

"Mom?"

In an instant, Phil was forgotten.

Hallie lay on her side on a sticky vinyl couch in the waiting room, her knees drawn up beneath her chin, her eyes fixed and empty. Her eyes frightened Dan the most, eyes that had gone hollow with grief. Her hair was matted in sodden clumps, and her hands were streaked with blood. Twice a nurse had gently suggested she wash up and had been ignored. Hallie hadn't spoken a word in the two hours since they'd arrived.

Dan sat on the floor in front of her, his hand resting on her arm, his shirt covered in blood, his arms swathed in bandages. He'd seen it all from the concession stand where he'd stopped for a burger after he'd claimed his keys and wallet from a bathhouse locker. It was a familiar sight to anyone who lived and worked near the beach— the darkening sky and the squall line sweeping in from the west. His lifeguard instinct had kicked in, and he'd headed back toward the pier. By the time he'd reached the water's edge, everyone had fled the concrete breakwater except for Miss V and Hallie.

The fall had crushed Mona's skull as the waves slammed her to the pavement and swept her onto the rocks. He'd watched the pummeling blows as she lay wedged between the concrete slabs that split her scalp in three places as he'd raced across the sand and scrambled out onto the jagged slabs. He had done his best to stanch the bleeding as he'd struggled to keep her head above water, but the waves had tossed them both like rag dolls. Before it was over, his blood and hers had flowed as one.

The Coast Guard personnel and the EMTs had commended his efforts as they'd rolled her body away and bandaged his wounds. It wasn't the first time they'd seen the lake take its toll.

He'd ridden beside Hallie in the ambulance and watched as she'd stroked her aunt's bloodied face. He never heard the shriek of the siren, only the screams of silence from the lifeless body and a shattered child.

It was one o'clock when Elsie appeared in the doorway of the family waiting room. For the first time in hours, Hallie moved, reaching for Dan's hand and letting him pull her to her feet. In an instant, she was embraced in Elsie's arms as the old woman whispered into the mass of Hallie's hair. Dan lifted himself slowly onto a chair and picked at the stains on his shirt where he had wiped his hands after it was all over.

A nurse appeared at the door, a young woman dressed in floral scrubs with a picture of two small children clipped to the ID tag that hung around her neck. She paused a moment before she stepped into the room and gently laid a hand on Elsie's arm.

"Family?"

"Yes." There was a ring of steel in the tone.

"This way, please."

Elsie nodded and followed, taking Hallie by the hand and guiding her through the swinging waiting-room doors. The nurse hesitated for a moment and nodded toward Hallie.

"Are you sure she's up to this?"

Elsie squared her shoulders and drew Hallie closer.

"No, I don't s'pose she is, but her God is. We'll be doin' this together, Hallie 'n' me. Just as soon as you can show me to a restroom where I can get this child cleaned up."

The nurse nodded and pointed to a restroom down the hall.

Dan watched from the waiting room as Elsie's arm encircled Hallie's waist and the doors swung shut behind them.

Chapter Nineteen

The light through the stained-glass windows illuminated the mauve carpet in waves of royal blue, scarlet, and gold. Hallie stared at the shifting patterns between the first row of white pews and the square oak lectern that stood at the front of the chapel beneath the vaulted wooden ceiling. The room was small, boasting only a half-dozen rows of benches, and she had chosen a seat in the second row on the left-hand side. Aunt Mona had always been a left-side sitter, and it seemed in those early morning hours that if Hallie had chosen a seat on the right, the universe itself might have tilted.

She was sure Elsie didn't know where she was. Or her mother or Dan, for that matter. And when she had slipped from the room and her mother's screams had overtaken her heart at the doctor's words, she hadn't known where she would go. She only knew she couldn't be there in that room, listening as the sentence was pronounced.

She wasn't sure how she'd found her way to the chapel. She'd been in this hospital once before, one summer when Stacy and she had been visiting Aunt Mona and they'd accompanied her to the hospital to visit Mrs. Byle from down the street. They'd bought a bouquet of fresh flowers from the hospital gift shop, and Aunt Mona had purchased bags of M&M's for each of them. Hallie remembered batting inflated latex gloves across the room, gloves Aunt Mona had taken from a box on a shelf, blown up, and tied so they could entertain Mrs. Byle with the wonders of slow-motion soccer. The same kind of box that sat on a small Formica stand near Aunt Mona's lifeless body.

At the rear of the room, Hallie heard the soft brush of the door against the carpet. She didn't turn to see if she'd been found. She would know soon enough if someone had come to claim her and force her from the dimly lit womb back into the maelstrom of reality.

Her feet were drawn up onto the pew, and her chin rested against her bare knees. Her arms encircled her legs, and it wasn't until her hands began to cramp that she loosened her grip enough for the blood to flow through her arms. Her eyes burned, and her lids were heavy, swollen slits from the crying, but something inside her refused to let them close. She felt somehow that if she blinked for even a moment too long, the world might shift again and collapse. She sat stone still, allowing the silence to stroke her soul, knowing the pain would come. Like a foot that has fallen asleep, the numbness gave way in flickering flashes of pain that rose and crescendoed as words tumbled from her soul.

There is nothing left of me, God. You've taken it all. I'm dead inside.

Her lips moved silently. The colors dancing on the carpet reminded her that the sun had risen once again, startling her with the insult that the world outside was somehow still spinning.

I can't do this. There's nothing in me that can bear this pain.

She pressed her hands into her eyes until shards of light shot through the darkness.

I thought that I had come to the end of myself, that there was nothing left in me that could care or hope, but I was wrong. Hope brought me to Aunt Mona the day I ran away, and hope brought me here this morning. Hope that You're there and that You're listening, that You care about the pain that's so great inside of me, that I don't know how to take the next breath.

She drew in a ragged sip of air and held it for a moment. Then she closed her eyes.

If You're really chasing me, I give up. You've won. I'm dropping dead in my tracks right now, right here, and You'll have to pick me up to ever move me from this place. I'm asking You to carry me because I can't see the next step or even if there's a path.

Her hands reached to her neck, and she fingered the heart-shaped necklace that fell from the slender chain

I used to believe You loved me. Please show me how to believe it again.

Behind her, the sound of gentle breathing pulled

her thoughts back into the room. Hallie opened her eyes and turned to look.

Dan sat in a pew two rows behind her. Someone had brought him a clean shirt, and a Styrofoam box sat on the bench next to him. He gestured toward it as he spoke.

"I thought you might need something. You haven't eaten since yesterday."

Hallie reached into her pocket and pulled an object from it, clasping it between her hands and staring at it. One hand flickered to her face, and she drew her palm across her forehead.

"I do need something, Dan, and I don't even know how to ask, so I'll just say it. I need you to pray with me, to pray for me. I don't have any words left, and I need to borrow some from a friend."

She watched as Dan rose slowly and made his way up the center aisle and seated himself beside her, never taking his eyes off her as he moved. He sat silently for a moment before speaking.

"In the end, Hallie, all the pain, the suffering, the injustice in the world come down to two questions: who is God, and can you trust Him?"

The questions hung in the air between them.

"Not when I look at my life. All I see is pain and betrayal and people hurting each other."

"And is that all you really think there is?"

The question reverberated in Hallie's heart, and she opened her fist and fingered the small motorcycle that lay in her hand. The answer came from deep within her, and her voice broke as she spoke.

"No."

"And is that a starting place for you? A starting place toward God?"

"Maybe."

"Then *maybe* is where we'll start."

Dan never thought to ask Hallie about the die-cast motorcycle she'd clutched in her hands as he'd prayed with her.

And he never thought to tell her about the words the doctor had spoken just moments after she'd fled her mother's screams. They were words he knew she had to hear from someone else, another time, another way.

Chapter Twenty

At first there was pain, unrelenting and suffocating, then a numbing oblivion. Shadows and light swirled in a mesmerizing cadence, rising and falling, then fading to blackness. In the distance, muffled sounds swelled and exploded in a cacophony of sound. Somewhere in the oblivion, shadows hovered silently on the edges of perception.

Then came the shimmering light, and once again, gold and rose tumbled together as the numbing oblivion segued to searing pain. The shadows teased, their voices drifting and echoing on the edge of sound, just beyond reach. The pain crescendoed and waned, then crescendoed again before fading to black.

The darkness settled over her with paralyzing power, the darkness of oblivion, a terror both serene and sweet. It embraced her, holding her close until once again the pain seeped beneath the jagged edges, dragging her again to the extremities of awareness.

And it was in one brilliant crescendo of pain that the shadows slipped away and a face flickered into Mona's consciousness.

Ellen's face, crying.

Ellen's voice, whispering.

And Ellen's fingers gently stroking her cheek.

Sounds drifted into Mona's dreams, tugging at the corners of her consciousness. They washed over her in gentle, swirling waves, and she fondled each awakening sensation, then released it to wait for the next like a child who sets down one toy to reach for another.

The squeak of rubber shoes approaching, then receding down the hallway.

The persistent beep of an IV monitor.

Faint voices of a morning weather report emanating from a room across the hall.

Each sound was a gift, her reassurance that she could hear, could think, could once again touch the world around her. From the first moments of her awakening, she had embraced the noises, the smells, even the pain, every thread of sensation that connected her to life.

She inhaled softly, drawing in the fragrance of the hyacinths. The first bouquet had come days before she'd begun to awaken after the craniotomy, when the swelling in her exposed brain had peaked and then finally plateaued. A bright-eyed young nurse had told her about the flowers one afternoon as she'd spooned Jell-O into Mona's mouth between reading cards on the assorted plants and sprays. The sweetness of the hyacinths had hung in the room for days before she had stirred to the sound of Ellen's voice and the awareness that someone was stroking her hand. Days later, Hallie had read the card to her, smiling as she'd spoken Adam's name. He'd stopped by the beach house to chat, the bold, black letters had explained, and a neighbor passing down the lane had told him about the accident. He wished God's best for her and would be praying. A fresh arrangement of mixed flowers and hyacinths had arrived every five days after that, signed simply *Prayers, Adam.* Hallie had made certain they were separated from the bank of flowers in the window nook—bouquets from former students, Gilead neighbors, Stewartville friends, and a philodendron from Trina's Café—and were placed on Mona's tray table near her Bible, directly in her line of vision.

Mona breathed deeply again and drank in the sweet fragrance of coconut lotion that rose from her shoulders and teased her memory with faded gray images. Ellen massaging her arms and legs with the silky liquid, using tentative strokes that had grown stronger as the weeks had passed. Ellen sleeping in a crumpled heap at the foot of her bed or thumbing through the Bible Elsie had placed on the bedside table. Ellen and Hallie huddled together in the recliner, entwined yet somehow barely touching. Ellen standing at the window, shrouded in a cloud of alcohol, watching for the husband who never came.

Even with her eyes shut tight against the morning, Mona knew that across the room Ellen was waking from her nightly vigil. Like so many hospital secrets, the bright-eyed nurse had revealed this one. In the first days, when everyone had gathered to wait for the death that never came, Ellen had slept each night on the foot of Mona's bed. The ritual had continued even after the coma had released its grip and the ventilator had been pulled from her throat. Ellen's awkward good-bye was conducted each night—a pat on Mona's hand and a quick kiss on the forehead before she hurried from the room. But each night between midnight and one, Mona would listen for the door to swing quietly open and for Ellen to slip into the arms of the recliner in the corner shadows. And in the morning, just before dawn, she would listen again for the door to open and for her sister to slip away. Neither of them had ever spoken of it.

Mona breathed in the scent of Chanel hanging in the air. She knew that in a moment Ellen would quietly gather her things to leave. And she knew that in the afternoon, when she returned, Ellen would pretend she hadn't been there through the night, and Mona would pretend that she had slept as her sister sat silently and riffled through her Bible into the late-night hours.

A spring groaned, accompanied by the creak of vinyl against vinyl, and Mona's pulse quickened. She willed herself to keep her breathing slow and steady as she chose her words. It would be so easy to lie still, to do nothing. But in a moment, Ellen would disappear into the early morning darkness for the last time, and when she returned later with Hallie, everything would be different.

A muffled rattle of keys stirred the silence as Ellen's purse was lifted from the floor. Mona listened as the light padding of footsteps counted away the seconds. The scent of perfume drifted across the room.

She opened her eyes when the door opened softly, watching as her sister stood silhouetted in the doorway, the hall lights shining softly beyond her. Her shoulders rose and fell in a gentle rhythm. Mona knew she was waiting, and she quietly cleared her throat. But Ellen's words came first, in an uneven whisper.

"Get your rest, Mona VanderMolen. It's a two-hour ride to Stewartville." Her eyes flickered to Mona's face and held there.

Mona felt the knot in her throat.

"Thank you, Ellen."

Ellen slipped her purse over her shoulder and dropped her gaze to the floor, her blonde hair falling forward and covering her eyes.

"Nothing you've ever done has ever meant this much to me, Ellen. Watching over me, being here, especially here . . . where I know it's hardest for you to be."

Mona watched as her sister's shoulders rose, then fell. Her breathing seemed to stop for a moment, and Mona saw the pain in her eyes. For a moment, her hand drifted to her eyes and then fell again as she lifted her head and nodded slowly. Then she turned to go, and the door slipped shut behind her.

She had not spoken, but Mona had heard.

Hallie arrived at nine, bursting through the door and plopping into the vinyl recliner, white shorts and peach cotton T showing off her deep tan.

"You ready to blow this pop stand, Auntie Em?"

Mona gestured to the bulging plastic bags piled on the foot of her bed.

"Ready? Do you know that this hospital serves

five different flavors of Jell-O, and that if you stack the cubes very carefully, you can build a replica of Shakespeare's Globe Theatre? And do you know how many games you can play with an inflated rubber glove, a couple of wads of gauze, and a spool of surgical tape? And did you know that if you can get your hands on a good, hot cup of tea just before they check vitals, you can actually freak out the nurses? I'm thinking of using my knowledge to author a book on ways to amuse yourself in hospitals to support me in my old age. And where is your mother, I might add?"

Hallie kicked off a sandal and surveyed what appeared to be a freshly pedicured foot.

"She's stopping for a few boxes of Godiva and some fresh fruit and pastry trays for the nursing staff, so I had Dan bring me. Actually, he's down the hall waiting to be reassured that you're decent so he can come say good-bye."

Mona reached for a navy blue West Shore High School baseball cap on her nightstand and slipped it on over the yellow bandanna she'd tied around her head. With the flourish of a television model, she gestured toward the navy chinos and yellow blouse she was wearing.

"And what do you think of the bandanna-hat combination with this festive home-going ensemble that Elsie brought me? Should I wear it or just throw pride to the wind and flash my red stubble?"

Hallie cocked her head to one side and smiled. "You're beautiful, Aunt Mona. The hottest Hollywood stars pale before your ravishing baldness. I can see it now—all the Stewartville women shaving their heads and wearing do-rags to keep up with you."

Mona reached for her purse on the tray table and pulled out a mirror as Hallie laughed.

"You're making fun of me, Hallie Bowen. You know, you might consider shaving your head as a sign of emotional support like some people do."

"Not on your life. Just envision that yearbook picture in a couple months. Now just sit there and be gorgeous while I go and get Dan."

Hallie disappeared out the door, and Mona inched herself to the side of the bed and slid her feet into leather huaraches. Then she reached up, running her fingers along the half-inch brush of stubble at the base of her neck, and sighed as she tried to calculate how long it might be before she would need a hairbrush again.

A gentle knock sounded, and Dan's head poked around the door.

"All right if I come in for a minute?" He smiled broadly as he stepped through the doorway, followed by a grinning Hallie.

"I'd sooner be hog-tied and thrown in a manure spreader than go home without seeing you, Dan," Mona said as she waved him in. "A little saying I learned from Elsie," she laughed as she watched

261

his eyes grow wide. She scooted back and leaned on her pillows as the two settled on the end of her bed.

"So how is my favorite hero, the man I owe my life to?"

Dan squirmed. "I'm fine, Miss V. I don't mind being on your list of favorites, but I'm not much in the way of a hero. You look wonderful."

Mona laughed. "What a wonderfully sweet lie. My stunning good looks have been dealt a serious blow, and my skull looks like something from a horror movie. But most days I know my name and which end of the fork to use, and I'm grateful."

Mona fluffed the pillows behind her and settled back.

"So give me an update on Hallie here. I know she's been spending a lot of time at Gilead with you and your friends when she's not up here driving the nurses crazy and hanging out with her dilapidated old aunt. I can see she's gotten a pretty good tan in the past six weeks, and I also hear she's developed a killer serve. Anything else I should know about?"

Mona watched with interest as Dan glanced sideways.

"I'm sure Hallie can speak for herself. I thought she'd have filled you in a little by now."

"Oh, really? So should I be getting excited or nervous?" Mona crossed her arms and looked at Hallie. "Want to shed any light here?"

262

Hallie shrugged her shoulders. "I don't know what the big deal is. I've been going to some Bible studies, hanging out with some kids, asking some questions."

"Questions?" Mona's tone was calm and deliberate, but she felt an exhilaration rising in her chest.

"Yeah."

"Been getting any answers?" Mona glanced back at Dan, searching for clues in his expression, but his eyes told her nothing.

"Maybe."

Mona waited as Hallie hesitated and looked down, plucking at the white cotton blanket.

"I guess the biggest answer I have right now is that I don't have any answers. That they have to come from someone bigger than I am."

"What kind of answers? And what kind of someone?"

Hallie continued plucking. "You know—answers to life stuff. Why we're here and . . . and where we're going. Whether there's any reason for all the . . . garbage."

Mona's chest grew tighter. In the weeks since she'd awakened from the coma, she had perceived an awakening in Hallie's spirit, and she'd watched and waited.

"So what are your thoughts on all those things, Hallie?"

Hallie looked up, and her gaze locked on

Mona's. For a moment, Mona was sure that the blood stopped flowing through her veins, and her heart stood still.

"Some kids at Gilead are helping me with that—some of Dan's friends. They know a lot about the Bible, and that's where I'm looking for answers. Right now, I'm working on figuring out what it means to be this."

She reached toward her neck and pulled Stacy's necklace from beneath her shirt.

"The stones spell out the word *dearest* because you wanted something as simple as a necklace to tell the world how much you loved your family. I'm working on believing that I'm really dear to God, that He could really love me so much that He came running after me when I'd done so many awful things."

Mona forced herself to breathe evenly and choose her words carefully. The knot was nearly choking her, and she tried to swallow it away.

"All those days I was lying there and couldn't speak or even open my eyes, I could feel you here with me, you and your mother. In those days, I was only afraid of one thing—that I might never see you and your mom come to love the God I love so much, that I might never see you understand what forgiveness is and how it frees us. I asked God for only one thing—for you to both become who God created you to be."

Hallie reached across the blankets and rested her

hands on top of Mona's hands. Mona drew in a long breath as she felt the pressure of Hallie's fingers squeeze her own and watched the tears flow freely down her face and drip onto the white hospital blanket. Mona reached out and gathered her into her arms, Hallie's hair sweeping the tears from her own cheeks.

"It's okay, Hal. All the answers you'll ever need are there for you to find—they've been there since the dawn of eternity, just like the promise of forgiveness. If Stacy could talk to you right now, she'd tell you you're forgiven by God, by her. She'd tell you to place your trust in the God who forgave her and then discover who the forgiven Hallie really is."

Mona whispered the words into Hallie's ear as she cradled her in her arms and rocked her gently.

"But I think I'm already beginning to see the forgiven Hallie. Am I right?" Mona pulled back and lifted Hallie's quivering chin.

The tears were streaming from Hallie's eyes and down her sunburned cheeks as Mona cupped her face in her right hand.

"Yes," Hallie whispered. "Glimpses."

In that moment, Mona knew that Hallie's heart had softened, and the glimpses would soon give way to wide-eyed wonder. Dan stood silently watching, the smile still playing on his lips.

"I think we have someone here to thank. Someone who's watched over you from the very start."

Mona directed her gaze to Dan. Tears choked her voice as she reached for his hand.

"You know there's no possible way I can thank you for everything—for me, for Hallie. For showing her what a real friend is. I owe you more than I can put into words.

"God has great things in store for you, Dan. Not because of what you've done, but because you know who God made you to be, and you're becoming more of that person every day. Your friendship to me and my family is a treasure beyond words. Thank you."

She pulled him into her arms and hugged him briefly, then leaned over and pulled an envelope from the top drawer of her nightstand.

"That's about enough of an old woman's emotion. There's something I want you to do. This is a thank-you card from me and from Hallie, too. We want you to promise not to read it until you're home tonight with your mother. Deal?" She took his hand and placed the card in it.

Dan stared at the card for a moment before he looked up.

She leaned forward and rested a hand on his. "It's just an old, bald woman's thank-you, Dan. You don't have to be afraid of it."

He shook his head as he slid the card into the pocket of his khaki cargo shorts.

"I only did what anybody would have done, Miss V. And Hallie was there every second."

"Yes, I know she wouldn't leave my side." Mona stroked Hallie's cheek, still wet with tears.

Dan broke the mood as he rose from the bed.

"This is amazingly rude of me, but I have to be going. I have a guarding shift this morning in fifteen minutes, and they can't open the pool until I get there. But now I have an excuse to drive to Stewartville soon and visit."

"Then give me a proper hug good-bye." Mona gathered him again into a warm embrace.

"Thank you," she whispered into his ear. She felt an almost imperceptible nod of his head, then watched as he straightened himself and walked toward the door.

"I'll see myself out. My prayers are with you in your recovery, Miss V. You're much loved." He smiled in Hallie's direction. "And we've already said good-bye, right?"

Hallie faced the door, and Mona saw only the curve of her cheek as she nodded. By the time Mona glanced back toward Dan, he was gone. Hallie turned slowly back to face her.

"I'm going to miss him. A lot, I think."

Hallie was quiet for a moment, and the silence hung in the air as if time were holding its breath. The lilt of a familiar lullaby drifted over the intercom, a musical announcement that, a floor above them, a child had been born. Hallie rose and walked to the door, closing it softly. Mona read a quiet resolve on her face as she returned and settled herself cross-legged on the end of the bed.

"Mom's coming soon. There's no time left."

Mona smoothed the blanket in front of her, then rested her hands lightly on the white surface. Even before she spoke, she knew there weren't enough words to say what needed to be said.

"I'm going to miss you, Hal, more than I could ever say, and I can't go home until I know you're all right."

Something flickered in the shadows of Hallie's eyes.

"I'm all right."

"And what does that mean?" Mona searched her face.

"I guess it means that there are a lot of things that were in my heart that aren't there anymore. Things I needed to give up. Things God wanted to take out."

The shoulders shifted again as Hallie's hand rose to her throat. She touched the delicate gold heart set with gemstones.

"Now what about you, Aunt Mona?"

Mona felt Hallie's eyes sweeping her face.

"I can't go home until I know you're all right, too."

Mona swallowed as Hallie slipped her hand into the pocket of her shorts and pulled out a silver wedding band.

"Forgiveness is a choice, right? Do you really believe it?"

Mona stared at the ring in Hallie's extended hand, then closed her eyes as scenes flashed through her memory.

Her mother weeping in an empty bedroom.

Ellen, barely a toddler, huddled in a corner, cringing beneath a verbal beating. The sound of slamming doors and heavy footsteps pounding down memory's corridor.

But the question of forgiveness was one she had settled with a tear-stained Bible open in her lap in the arms of her mother's rocker just days before the accident.

"Yes, Hallie, forgiveness is a choice."

Mona slipped the chain bearing her mother's band from around her neck, the chain the paramedics had removed and nurses had returned when Mona had awakened and asked for it.

She held it out to Hallie, who grasped one end while she held the other. They sat quietly for a moment, the silver strand suspended between them, before Mona nodded. Hallie carefully placed the wide band over her end of the chain and slid the ring to the center until it nested against the smaller silver band. Then, slowly, Mona turned as Hallie draped the chain around her neck and fastened the clasp.

Moments later when Ellen arrived, the two were busy tucking cards and gifts into a plastic hospital bag. But Mona's mind was preoccupied with two things.

Her real home-going gifts: gratitude and hope.

Chapter Twenty-One

Mona awoke to the rustling of pages riffling through her dreams. She opened her eyes and blinked against the first rays of sunlight peeking through her open bedroom window as she raised her head. The alarm clock read 6:10 AM, and she rolled slowly back onto her pillows as Oscar nuzzled closer. Again the gentle breeze skimmed the surface of the open book on the marble-topped bedside stand and fingered its pages, and she closed her eyes and smiled.

Just five more minutes, she told herself as she listened to the sounds of the morning unfolding below her window. Somewhere down Mercantile Street, a car door slammed. *Trina heading into the café to get a start on the morning baking.* In the distance, a dog barked, and Mona envisioned old Fred Simpson and his ancient greyhound, Doobie, heading out for their morning walk. A car approached, then slowed and stopped at the only light Stewartville boasted, the light that set it apart from Huddleston and Parmenter and other nearby villages. Someone called a hello from the street below, and a horn tooted lightly as the car passed through the intersection.

Beneath the crumpled sheet, Mona heard a gentle whine, and she rolled her eyes. She groaned as she slowly eased into a sitting position and slid her feet into the huaraches that she'd kicked beneath the edge of the bed the night before. Then she reached for the cane hooked over the towel bar on the marble-topped nightstand.

"You don't make morning easy, Oscar. Lucky for you, I need the therapy."

She slipped her arms into the familiar pink robe Hallie had brought to her in the hospital as Oscar nosed out from under the covers and gave his ears an energetic flapping. Then she gathered the dog under one arm and lowered him to the floor.

Mona sat for a moment on the edge of the bed before she stood slowly and leaned her weight into the cane. She could feel the heaviness in her left leg as she made her way across the hardwood floor, stepping carefully with her right foot and focusing on her balance. She gauged the numbness and tingling in the leg against previous days, searching for indications that the pinpricks had lessened and the wooden numbness had decreased. But before she'd made it halfway to the door, she knew the answer.

In the two weeks since she'd come home from the hospital, there'd been no change.

She reached the landing outside the apartment and hung the cane from the neck of her robe as she grasped the railings on either side to ease herself down the stairway. Oscar watched from the landing, his head cocked to one side, until she reached the bottom step and called for him.

"Don't make me come up there to get you if you want to live another day."

She grasped the cane again in her left hand as Oscar scrambled down the stairs, then she weaved slowly toward Harold's workroom through an assortment of piecrust tables, sewing stands, and other vintage reproductions.

"The man does beautiful work, you have to admit, Oscar. And since Elsie started stocking his pieces last month, every bed-and-breakfast and vintage hotel in the Midwest has wanted 'Dean's Distinctive Reproductions.' I do believe it's time to call Eskel Barkel and tell him he can take a flying leap."

Mona made her way slowly through the back room while Oscar pranced in circles. She opened the back door and watched him skitter into the alley. She leaned heavily against the doorframe as the miniature dachshund sniffed and scouted for the perfect spot in the familiar patch of grass near the Dumpster.

The sound of crunching gravel caught her attention, and Mona turned to see a familiar maroon Grand Marquis approaching down the dirt lane. A puff of lavender hair peeked above the steering wheel. The casual onlooker would have thought the vehicle was driverless, but everyone in Stewartville knew better. The car pulled to a stop just short of the back door of the shop.

"Get yourself back up to your room, Mona

VanderMolen, and I'll take care of that poor excuse for a dog. You need at least another hour of sleep before you head out to that auction you got no business goin' to in the first place."

The door heaved open, and Elsie emerged from the car in a turquoise and purple floral cobbler's apron with matching turquoise slacks and tennis shoes. Within seconds, she was scooting Mona through the back room and toward the stairs, waving her arms as if she were shooing flies.

"I'm not takin' no backtalk from you, girl. Jessica's bringing a sausage-and-egg casserole and cinnamon rolls 'bout eight, and I'll bring a plate up to you then. You crawl back into that bed and leave Oscar to keep me company while I finish up a little paperwork on orders comin' and goin' today. I can barely keep up with the reproduction orders, not to mention all the new people in and out now."

Elsie's hands were on her hips, and Mona knew she was defeated. She hung the cane once again from the neck of her robe and gripped the railings as she hoisted herself back toward the loft, muttering with each step. Elsie watched from the workroom doorway. With a final heave, Mona pulled herself to the landing and limped toward the apartment door.

"You know, Elsie, you're not always an easy woman, and some days I'm not sure I'm allowed to take my next breath unless you give the say-so."

273

She turned and saw Elsie's shoulders stiffen with a quick intake of breath.

"But no one takes care of me the way you do. You do things for me before I even know I need to do them myself. You protect me and sacrifice for me, and I don't think I tell you often enough how much it means to me and how much I love you."

The shoulders relaxed, and Elsie exhaled. "Well, then."

Mona smiled. "Well then to you, too. I'll see you at eight." She turned the knob and stepped into her apartment, closing the door softly behind her.

Leaning heavily on the cane, she made her way slowly across the bedroom, pausing in front of her mirrored, marble-topped Victorian dresser. She ran the fingers of her free hand through the inch-long spiky red stubble and studied the drawn lines of her face.

Despite Elsie's best efforts and two weeks of pampering, the pounds she had lost in the hospital had not returned, and she still looked pale and drawn. *But a few hours in the sun at today's auction will help put that straight,* she told herself as she turned and made her way toward her mother's rocker nestled between her nightstand and the window, which was open to the street below. Weeks of rehab in the hospital had told her that the only places to look were forward toward the next goal and heavenward for the strength to get there.

Today's goal was to purchase a glass-front oak barrister's bookcase at another Meller auction.

She hooked her cane once again to the rail of the nightstand and lowered herself slowly into the chair. Beside her, a small leather book lay open, a letter wedged between its pages. It had come just days after she'd arrived back in Stewartville, and she'd pored over it often when she needed a reminder of things that were truly important. She reached for the book and slipped the letter from its pages, then began to read:

Dear Miss V,

I can't describe to you the shock of opening your letter and realizing what you and Hallie had done. Neither my mother nor I will ever be able to express our appreciation for your act of kindness in helping to find a corporate sponsor for my college education. I have never felt that I acted as a hero the day I helped you on the pier. It should be a natural thing for all of us to run to help others, especially people who have always done so themselves.

Please thank Hallie's father on our behalf for seeking out a sponsor for me through his contacts as a financial investor. It was a most gracious and generous thing for him to do. We are overwhelmed at the way God has woven together the lives of so many people to accom-

plish something far greater than we could ever have dreamed.

My mom and I plan to come to Stewartville just as soon as you're stronger so we can deliver our thanks in person. We hope that will be soon. In the meantime, we're keeping a close eye on Hallie and her mother. They seem to be enjoying their time alone at the beach house, and I see them often swimming together or sunning. Hallie's spoken a few times with me about her father's desire for a divorce, and she's continuing to come to Bible studies at Gilead and is asking a lot of questions. I even saw her mother at one of the evening concerts. She and Hallie were sitting on a blanket in the grass together outside the Tabernacle. I don't remember who the musician was that night, but I do remember that they were listening and smiling.

You continue to be in my prayers, Miss V. May God continue to strengthen you in body and in spirit. Thank you again for helping me realize a dream.

With warmest regards,
Dan

Mona folded the letter and slipped it back between the pages of the small leather book, stroking the cover as she closed it. With her index finger, she traced the gold embossing on the front cover: *1960*.

Her fingers traced the number over and over as she had done for days since she'd returned home. Today was the day she would open it. She whispered her prayer aloud, knowing she needed to hear the words that had echoed in her heart for so many days.

"Now it's my turn to listen, God. Let me hear my father on these pages—the words he somehow couldn't speak to us and the dreams he never shared. Help me to see him and love him, imperfections and all, just the way You see and love us all."

A breath of wind stirred the air as she sat with closed eyes. Then she opened the cover and began to read.

Mona ran her fingers through the soggy stubble that protruded from beneath her red bandanna as she fanned herself vigorously with a frayed straw hat. The temperature on the sign at the bank had read eighty-six degrees as she'd headed north up Oak Street, then west on Adams, but Elsie had made sure she'd come prepared. A water bottle hung from a clip secured to a belt loop on her jean shorts, and a cooler packed with mountains of ice, fresh fruit, sandwiches, raspberry iced tea, and a half-dozen Hershey's bars sat on the front seat of the F-150. Mona had been careful to slather herself with sunscreen and had even slipped her sunglasses into the front pocket of her white blouse before submitting herself to Elsie's inspection at the back door.

But six weeks in the hospital and two more under Elsie's watchful eye in the shop hadn't prepared her for standing for even an hour in the glaring heat of the late August sun. She'd made quick rounds of the auction merchandise and confirmed her suspicion that the only item of interest was the oak barrister bookcase, the bookcase she'd selected to display her father's diaries along the far wall of her apartment near her mother's rocker.

Auctioning off Mary Donegan's estate won't take long, she'd told herself as she'd read the flyer she'd received in the mail two weeks earlier. She'd known Mary from church and had been in her house dozens of times to pick up baked goods for the library sale or to gather with other women from Stewartville Community Church for Bible study. Mona had always admired the bookcase that sat in the front parlor, flanking the baby grand where Mary had supported herself for over fifty years by giving piano lessons to half the children in Stewartville.

Mona glanced around the tiny yard of Mary's pristine white bungalow, now crowded with vinyl kitchen chairs, a gold velour recliner, dressers and bedsteads, and an assortment of boxes piled high with linens, dishes, and blankets. Duane was working his way down the aisle of appliances that lined the narrow strip of driveway to the ancient clapboard garage Mary had used for a potting shed. Mona rubbed the thigh of her left leg and shifted her weight as she eyed the kitchen chairs. The one to the far right stood in a swath of shade beneath one of the towering maples that hemmed the front lawn between the sidewalk and the street. The three others were stacked with boxes of books.

Mona settled the straw hat back on her head and began to inch her way through the crowd toward the open chair, nodding and greeting friends as she passed, steeling herself against the growing pain in her leg and the pounding in her head.

Yes, I'm doing much better, Sharon. Thank you for your prayers. And Hallie's fine. With her mother at the beach house for a few more days until school starts.

The flowers were lovely, Ginny Mae. How wonderful of you to think of me.

Yes, the cane's a bit of a nuisance, but most days I'm glad to have it. Brain damage, the doctors tell me. No, we're not really sure yet. They tell me time will tell.

Perhaps Elsie had been right, she told herself as she leaned into the cane, willing her face into a thin smile. Maybe it had been too early to venture out by herself.

She gave a few final greetings as she worked her

way toward the chair, then eased herself into it, closing her eyes for a moment as the pain ebbed from her leg.

Thoughts of the beach house, of Ellen and Hallie, raced through her mind, and she envisioned herself in the scenes. The three of them eating lake perch and onion rings from take-out boxes along the channel wall. The three of them walking the trails through the woods at Hoffmaster State Park or climbing the dunes. The three of them talking or maybe just sharing the silence of a quiet evening on the deck of the beach house.

Mona's eyes opened as Duane's voice broke into her thoughts. He was moving on to the items on the front lawn, then on into the house for the larger items of furniture. With any luck, in an hour she would be home, where Elsie could fuss over her and she could rest in the air-conditioned comfort of her apartment.

But even as she thought it, Mona knew where she truly wanted to be: with Ellen and Hallie. She wanted to listen to the sound of the surf pounding on the shore, reminding her of the glory of God, who had graced her with a little more time—time to know her sister, time to know her niece.

Her hand drifted to her throat, and she fingered the two rings that nestled, one within the other, on the silver chain around her neck. Next week would be Ellen and Hallie's final week at the beach house before Hallie would return to school. And it would be Ellen's last week before returning to face divorce papers. Slowly, a plan began to take shape in Mona's mind. A weekend of quiet walks, dinners, and conversations, if Ellen would allow it. A farewell weekend for just the three of them. She reached for the side of her jeans where her cell phone hung from a clip.

"Are there any instructions I need today so I don't get myself into trouble?"

The strong male voice came from above her, and Mona moved her head slowly as she glanced up. Adam Dean stood behind her, his hands lightly gripping the back of her chair.

"I was wondering if there was anything here today I should know about that you have your eye on so I'm not accused of being a mercenary if I decide to bid."

Mona's mouth broadened into a wide grin, and she leaned forward onto the cane to stand, but Adam's hands moved to her shoulders, and he pressed her gently back into the chair.

"No need, Mona. You just rest right where you are."

She felt her face flush. In one fluid movement, he bent down and moved a box of hand-embroidered linens from the chair next to her to the top of a quarter-sawn oak washstand and sat beside her.

Mona felt the intensity of his gaze as he stared

for a moment and then smiled and cocked his head to one side.

"You are proof positive that God answers prayer, Mona VanderMolen. I'd heard you might never walk or speak again, but here you are."

Mona glanced toward the crowd. Several heads were turned in their direction as people watched with unmasked interest, and Ginny Mae was pointing and tugging so hard on her cousin Fonda's arm that Mona thought it might come clean off. Once again, she felt the warmth rush to her face.

"I'm not sure you could call my wobble a walk, but it eventually gets me where I want to go, praise God. And as for the talking, I guess you'll have to judge for yourself if God did the world a favor by giving that back to me."

Ginny Mae had edged closer, and Mona shook her head and giggled softly as she called out, "This is my friend Adam, Ginny Mae, who sent me buckets and buckets of flowers while I was in the hospital. A highly successful businessman, and unmarried, I might add."

Ginny Mae's hand flew to her mouth, and Mona laughed out loud.

Mona watched Adam's eyes grow wide.

"I might as well give her something to talk about. The town's been fairly parched for gossip since the big news of my homecoming. If there's one thing I learned as I camped out at death's door, it's that time is precious, and we shouldn't dance around wasting it.

"So, I want to thank you for the hyacinths, Adam. They were lovely. I could smell them for days before I even knew they were there."

Mona had glanced back at Adam's face, and the wide-eyed gaze had shifted to an amused intensity.

"Like an unseen presence surrounding you. A lot like God, don't you think?"

His words surprised her, and for a moment, she forgot to answer. A sudden smile had lit up his face, and she was suddenly intrigued to know the reason why.

"Uh . . . of course. I mean, yes."

He cleared his throat and glanced at Mona's cane.

"I stopped by the shop today for a delivery, and Elsie told me I could find you here. She was a little worried that you were overdoing it, and in my opinion, her instincts were right. You're looking a little worse for wear here."

Mona suddenly realized her left hand was kneading her thigh, and her head was still pounding.

"Sounds like you two are in cahoots. I was actually doing quite well until about ten minutes ago, and then this left leg of mine decided to mutiny and my brain began to melt into oatmeal. As to your earlier question, I was hoping to bid on a glass-front barrister bookcase for some special books I'd like to display."

A sudden exhaustion gripped her throat, as if the wind had been sucked from her lungs, and she felt her voice quaver.

"I guess I'm just not sure I'm going to hold out that long. I'm sorry, Adam. I think I may have overextended myself a bit. I think I could use a bit of a rest, and I have a phone call I need to make. If you could help me to my truck, the bookcase can wait. It's yours for the bidding."

Adam stood and extended his hands to her.

"I have a better idea. You lie down in the air-conditioned comfort of my truck and make your call and rest. I'll wait here and bid on your bookcase. Then I'll load it up and drive it back to the shop. I can walk back later and drive your truck home for you."

Mona felt the tears spring to her eyes, and she blinked them away. Since the brain injury, they had come with annoying regularity.

"I couldn't impose on you that way. Really, I don't want to be any trouble."

"There's nothing more I'd rather do right now."

He smiled, and suddenly Mona knew there was nothing she'd rather have him do than lead her somewhere where she could get out of the sun and concentrate on breathing.

"And I'm leaving you no choice. I promised Elsie I'd look out for you."

Adam reached for the cane and hooked it over his wrist, then took her hands in his own as he raised her to her feet. Mona gripped his arm and felt the whisper of his breath on her neck as he navigated her through the crowd toward the Suburban he'd double-parked in the street next to her truck. Mona was sure she heard Ginny Mae gasp as they passed.

He stopped as they reached the back door, and he turned slowly to face her.

"And what are you willing to offer?"

Mona's mind went blank for a moment.

"For the bookcase, Mona. What are you willing to pay? How much is it worth to you to have it?"

She stared into his eyes.

"You decide. I trust you."

Adam smiled. "Do you? Because I've already decided. Things of value don't come cheap, but when you see something that's worth the price, you need to know what it's worth to you to go after it. I've decided to start small and work my way up so I don't scare you off." He turned her toward the Suburban and opened the door.

The back seat was filled with hyacinths, their stems carefully wrapped in moist towels and slipped inside plastic bags.

"The last of the summer blooms. I thought they should be yours."

Their fragrance washed over her, and she closed her eyes and drew in a slow, deep breath. For a moment she felt as if her lungs would burst with the sweetness. Then she felt herself slowly exhale. She turned to look into his face, a growing realization burning in her heart.

"Why did you do this?"

"Because I owe you an apology, and an apology should be worthy of the circumstance and the person. In light of those two things, I also have a half-dozen Krispy Kremes in a bag on the front seat. Glazed. Nobody will ever say that Adam Dean doesn't know how to impress a woman."

Mona was suddenly, hilariously aware of the stubble on her head and the perspiration on her cheeks. She threw back her head and laughed, a laugh that bubbled up from deep within her. A pain shot through her leg, and she leaned hard into Adam's arm, pretending not to notice as heads turned. He slipped his hand around her waist as her leg gave way and her weight fell across his arm.

"Keep that up and we'll be the lead story in the 'Comings and Goings' column of the *Stewartville Sentinel* tomorrow," she whispered as she fought to catch her balance.

Adam's gaze was direct as he turned her to face him.

"With a laugh like that, Mona VanderMolen, I don't think I care."

A moment later, she found herself resting comfortably on the back seat of the Suburban, enveloped in the fragrance of hyacinths and the sound of her sister's voice welcoming her for a weekend visit at the beach house.

When they arrived at the shop an hour later, to unload the bookcase, Elsie was waiting at the alley door with Oscar in her arms, a look of unmasked delight on her face, and a box of vases at her feet.

And for the first time in a very long time, Mona felt that she had truly come home.

Center Point Publishing
600 Brooks Road ● PO Box 1
Thorndike ME 04986-0001 USA

(207) 568-3717

US & Canada:
1 800 929-9108
www.centerpointlargeprint.com